GRANNY GRABBERS'
Whizz Bang World

Charlotte Haptie

I[illegible]iamson

Hodder Children's Books

A division of Hachette Children's Books

First published in Great Britain in 2012
by Hodder Children's Books

1

A Catalogue record for this book is available from the British Library

ISBN 978 1 444 90408 6

Typeset in Weiss by Avon DataSet Ltd,
Bidford on Avon, Warwickshire

Printed and bound by CPI Group (UK) Ltd, Croydon, CR0 4YY

The paper and board used in this paperback by Hodder Children's Books
are natural recyclable products made from wood grown in
sustainable forests. The manufacturing processes conform to the
environmental regulations of the country of origin.

Hodder Children's Books
a division of Hachette Children's Books
338 Euston Road, London NW1 3BH
An Hachette UK company
www.hachette.co.uk

For Caroline Rose

and

Jacob and Harrie Porter

– Charlotte Haptie

To Maisie and Maddy Dodd

– Pete Williamson

Part One

1

Granny Grabbers Arrives

Granny Grabbers arrived at the front door of Delilah Smart's house on a sunny Monday morning in a large cardboard box. The postman didn't know what was inside, he just knew that it was very heavy and it kept beeping to itself.

Auntie Tillie was visiting at the time. She and Delilah went to the front door and Mrs Smart came rushing up the hall behind them.

'Oh, thank goodness,' said Mrs Smart. 'It's the childcare robot. It's come to look after Delilah. Isn't that wonderful?'

'This comes with it,' said the postman. 'And

could you sign here, please, on the dotted line.'

He gave Mrs Smart some bits of paper, and a book called *Instructions for the Use of Your Childcare Robot from Happy Home Robotics*.

Delilah stared at the box. It had just started rocking from side to side.

'It keeps doing it,' whispered the postman. 'We thought perhaps it was some sort of self-propelled pram.'

The box definitely made a deep buzzing noise and then a beep.

'With an alarm or hooter,' he added.

'Thank you so much,' said Mrs Smart firmly. 'That will be all.' And she shooed the postman off down the path and locked the door behind him. Then she clapped her hands in excitement and began tearing open the top of the box as if ten birthdays had come at once.

'What exactly is a childcare robot?' asked Auntie Tillie.

'A childcare robot is much more reliable

than a human,' said Mrs Smart breathlessly. 'It will provide the perfect conditions for Delilah to develop and be very good at everything as soon as possible. Just like I was. You know how her father and I both love competitions. Well, we want her to enter the Worldwide Junior Extreme General Knowledge Competition in the summer. Plus the robot will do all the housework.'

Auntie Tillie's mouth fell open. Her kindly eyes went as round as cereal bowls.

'All the other parents at the Big Brains Institute where we work have got one,' continued Mrs Smart, ignoring her. 'Some of them have got two. It feeds the child, washes its clothes—'

'Delilah is not an "it",' said Auntie Tillie. 'And a *machine* can't look after a child.'

'Don't be silly, Tillie. Help me finish unpacking it.'

Delilah stared at the childcare robot. It was

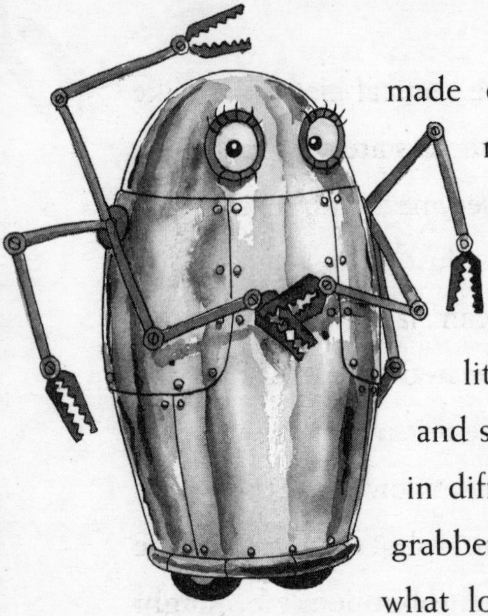

made out of chunky grey metal and shaped like a barrel with a round head that tilted and swivelled, no neck, little wheels underneath and six long arms pointing in different directions with grabbers on the end. It had what looked like headlamps in the sort of place where humans have eyes. They had fringed lids that went up and down.

'Hmm. I thought it would be slim and elegant, like me,' said Mrs Smart. 'It's a bit round, isn't it?'

'There's nothing wrong with being round,' said Tillie, who was a bit round herself.

She stared suspiciously at the robot. 'And what are *those?*' she added, pointing at the dark discs in the middle of the two headlamps.

'Oh, for goodness' sake, Tillie,' snapped Mrs

Smart. 'Those are the optical detectors, like eyes. The auditory detectors are on the sides.'

'You mean it can see me?' said Delilah in a very small voice.

'Yes, obviously it can. It can see and hear. It's a highly sophisticated piece of robotic technology. We wouldn't leave you in the care of just any machine, you know.'

Delilah looked the robot straight in the optical detectors. The robot looked straight back at her. Suddenly its headlamps glowed pink. It began to roll slowly towards her across the spotless polished floor.

'Aah!' cried Delilah.

Mrs Smart hadn't noticed. She was reading the instruction book.

The robot was getting closer and closer.

'What's it doing?' squeaked Delilah.

Auntie Tillie sprang into action. She stepped bravely in front of the robot and tried to push it back as hard as she could. The robot was very heavy and she might as well have tried to stop a battleship; but it was stopping anyway. It rattled to a halt just in front of Delilah and made a soft beeping sound.

Then it held out a grabber and put its head on one side.

Mrs Smart rustled through the instructions.

'I think it must be programmed to shake hands,' she said at last. 'Seems a waste of time to me. It doesn't talk. That would be expensive and unnecessary.'

Delilah swallowed. Very slowly, she held out her hand. She and the robot shook hand-to-grabber. The childcare robot blinked its headlamps.

'It says here that most customers like to give their robot a name,' said Mrs Smart. '"Because at first leaving your child in the care of a machine may seem a little cold."' She frowned. 'Oh, I think that's silly.'

'Well, I don't,' said Auntie Tillie.

Mrs Smart went on reading. '"Long fibres protect the headlamps and look like eyelashes . . . your robot is devoted to the care of your child and to doing the housework. The headlamps should be pink at all times. If they change colour this means that the robot is having Feelings and Ideas. Send it back to us at Happy Home Robotics at once. Feelings and Ideas lead to trouble. They also drain energy from household task circuits."'

At that moment the robot spun round on its

little wheels, banged into the wall and trundled off purposefully down the hall. Auntie Tillie and Delilah crept after it.

The robot arrived at the bottom of the stairs. Surely these would be a challenge: after all, it was shaped like a barrel with little wheels underneath. Not ideal for climbing stairs.

It rocked from side to side. Then it rose upwards, just a few centimetres. The little wheels lifted clear of the floor.

'Oh my,' said Auntie Tillie. 'It's got springs.'

The robot was indeed now standing on a lot of springs. They were just visible underneath it. It began to bounce up and down, very slightly, beeping to itself. Then it shot up the stairs two at a time. The whole house seemed to shake. Delilah and Auntie Tillie gasped and clung on to each other.

They heard the robot rattling and creaking from room to room above them. Then it appeared at the top of the stairs, looked down and beeped very quietly . . .

'I think it's scared', whispered Delilah.

The robot closed its headlamps tight, clasped all of its grabbers together, swayed alarmingly – and launched itself off the top step.

Faster and faster.

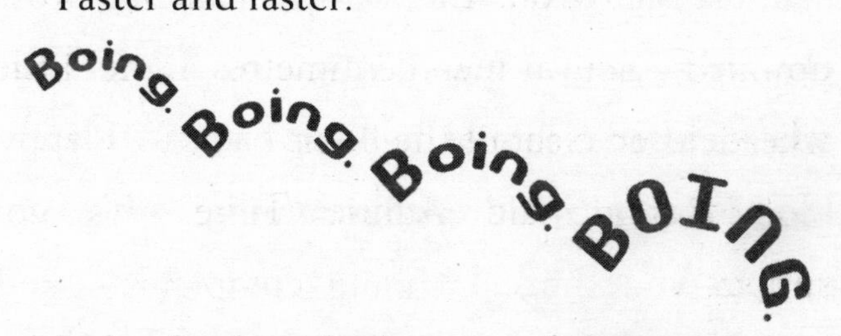

It was back at the bottom of the stairs.

'Wow,' said Delilah, much impressed.

But the robot hadn't finished yet. It had brought a few things down from the bathroom. Whirring and buzzing with efficiency, it extended two grabbers holding hairbrushes and two more holding combs, and very quickly brushed and combed Delilah's hair into a new and original style involving spiky bits in all directions. Finally and thrillingly it sprayed her with some of Mrs Smart's very, very expensive perfume.

'Thanks,' said Delilah.

She looked into the robot's optical detectors. They turned a darker, rosier shade of pink, which was interesting because Mrs Smart had just said that if the robot's headlamps ever changed colour it meant it was having feelings and ideas and should be sent back to Happy Home Robotics for reprogramming.

'Do you think I should complain?' asked Mrs Smart, coming down the hall with the instruction book. 'I've found a spelling mistake in here.'

Auntie Tillie rolled her eyes at the robot.

The robot looked politely at the floor.

'I think your electrical nanny needs a name,' said Auntie Tillie. 'You know what I'm going to call her? Granny Grabbers.' She whispered into what she hoped was an auditory detector on the side of the robot's head, 'You look after our Delilah, sweetheart. Her mum and dad don't have a clue.' And she winked.

Granny Grabbers' headlamps flashed from polite pink to a wild and exciting red. Just for a moment. Then she winked back.

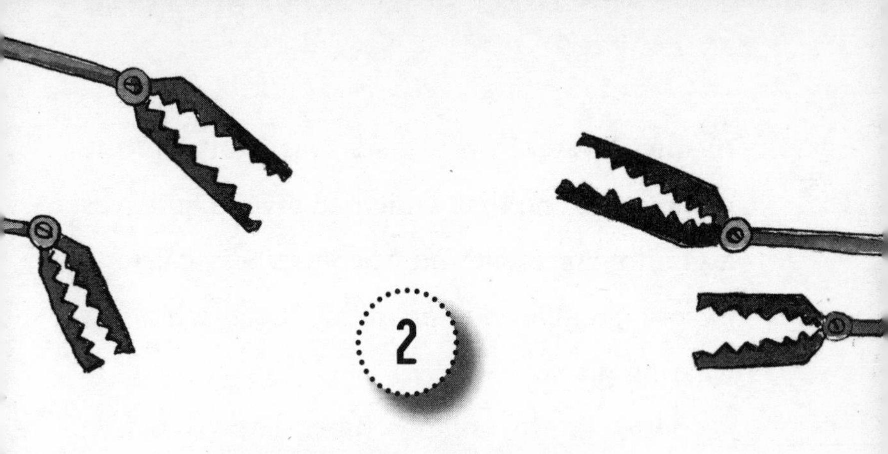

2

Sir Isaac Newton

The next morning it was time for Auntie Tillie to go home. She and Granny Grabbers were in the garden with Delilah. Delilah was sitting in a tree and Auntie Tillie had a deckchair. Granny Grabbers couldn't sit because she didn't bend in the middle, so she stayed standing up, with all three pairs of grabbers neatly clasped on her chest.

Hercules, the big white cat from next door, came and sniffed Granny Grabbers' wheels.

It was a lovely quiet moment in the sunshine.

Then Mr and Mrs Smart came bouncing out

of the house. Mrs Smart was carrying the computer game that Tillie had given Delilah as a goodbye present and Mr Smart was carrying a very strange-looking teddy bear who was wearing glasses.

'Look at this simply super Brain Building Bear we've got for you, Delilah,' yelled Mrs Smart. 'It's much better than the computer game you gave her, Tillie. You must take that back. It isn't educational.'

Granny Grabbers' headlamps flashed an angry lime green.

Delilah jumped down from the tree.

'Isn't she a bit big for another teddy bear?' asked Auntie Tillie.

'It's a special sort of bear,' said Mrs Smart, snatching the bear from Mr Smart and waving it about. 'It's called the Sir Isaac Newton Brain Building Alphabet Bear. Sir Isaac Newton was this incredibly famous scientist, Tillie. You won't have heard of him.'

'I most certainly have heard of him,' muttered Auntie Tillie.

'Squeeze his middle, Delilah,' said Mr Smart. 'It's not difficult. When the man in the shop had shown me a couple of times I got the hang of it straight away.'

Mrs Smart handed the bear to Delilah. He was big and solid, with short grey fur, a disapproving expression and large glasses with green plastic frames. She squeezed his tummy.

'A is for artichoke,' announced the bear solemnly, 'arthropod and anchovy.'

'Goodness me! That's a bit complicated,' exclaimed Auntie Tillie.

'Don't be silly, Tillie—' began Mr Smart.

'We want Delilah to start building her brain immediately,' interrupted Mrs Smart. Then she added, in a much quieter voice, which only Mr Smart was supposed to hear, 'What is an arthropod, darling? I seem to have forgotten.'

'Arthropods are creatures with a hard outside,' said Auntie Tillie casually. 'Like crabs.'

'And anchovies are little dogs that like pizza,' said Mr Smart. 'Everybody knows that.'

Suddenly an unexpectedly loud and rude-sounding squelchy buzzing noise echoed all around the garden. Auntie Tillie looked at Granny Grabbers, who was staring innocently at a flowerbed.

'Tillie, did you just blow a very rude raspberry?' demanded Mrs Smart.

'Certainly not,' said Tillie. 'It was probably just the cry of the lesser-spotted artichoke. I saw one fly past a couple of minutes ago.'

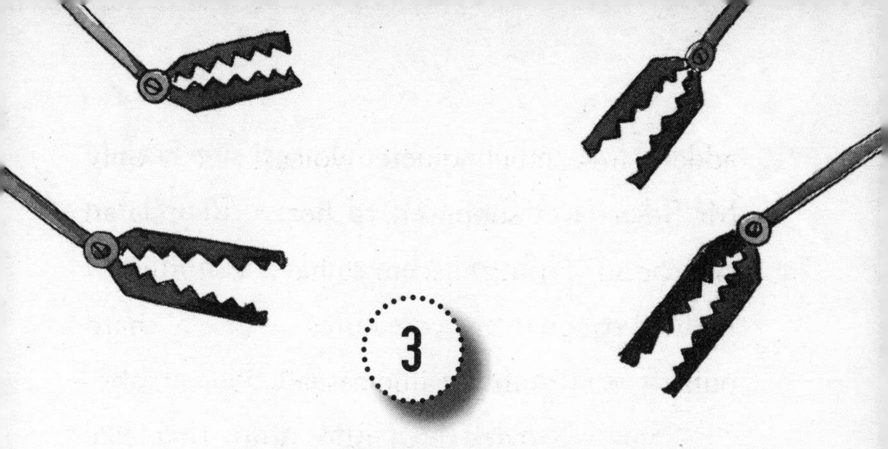

3

The Ugly Sisters

So Delilah had a robot to look after her and a very good thing it was too.

Mr and Mrs Smart rushed back to their important jobs at the Big Brains Institute. Every night when they came home, they rushed to the swimming pool and the Dinky Wrinkles Tanning Studios. At the weekends they worked out in their private gym.

They had entered Delilah in to the Worldwide Junior Extreme General Knowledge Competition. She tried to keep learning as many facts as possible. Mr and Mrs Smart quickly set up a special website called ourlittlesmartie.com to keep the world updated on her development. They put lots of photos of themselves on it.

A few weeks after Granny Grabbers arrived, Mrs Smart invited the people from the local television news to come and meet the family. She rushed out and bought everyone new clothes. Then she told Granny Grabbers to go into the cupboard under the stairs and stay there. Delilah watched horrified as Granny Grabbers disappeared into the dust and the dark and the door was closed firmly behind her.

As soon as the cameras arrived, Mr and Mrs Smart sat neatly on the sofa with Delilah squished in between them, hardly able to breathe.

'Your website has attracted a lot of interest,' said the lady from the local news programme. 'Why do you think your daughter is so advanced for her age?'

'She takes after me,' began Mrs Smart. 'I am incredibly intelligent and talented at lots of things.'

'We met doing a pantomime with the Big Brains Institute Amateur Players,' said Mr Smart quickly. 'My wife was the back end of a horse.'

'No, I wasn't,' said Mrs Smart.

'Oh yes you were,' said Mr Smart, smiling for the camera.

'We were Cinderella's sisters,' continued Mrs Smart, leaning towards him and pushing him so that she was in the picture instead. (Delilah almost completely disappeared.)

'The ugly ones?' prompted the journalist helpfully.

'He was very ugly,' said Mrs Smart. 'I was a little bit ugly, as the part requires, but in a beautiful way. Obviously.'

* * *

At last the television people went home and Mrs Smart texted all her friends to tell them about the interview.

Then she remembered to open the door of the cupboard under the stairs.

Granny Grabbers came hurtling out. She had been in there for two hours. She was covered in dust and she had a big cobweb dangling over her optical detectors. Her headlamps were extremely bright green. She was furious.

But Mrs Smart had never noticed that Granny Grabbers' headlamps changed colour and she didn't notice now. Otherwise she would have followed the instruction book and sent her back to Happy Home Robotics because coloured headlamps meant Feelings and Ideas.

Granny Grabbers barged into the living room. Delilah rushed up to her and kissed her on her nearest auditory detector.

Unfortunately, Mr Smart came striding in

holding the newspaper and spoilt it all.

'Look at this, Delilah,' he said. And he held up the horrible headline.

BABBATUNDE BOY GENIUS

Mr Smart started reading the paper out loud. 'Babbatunde is from the Island of Amania, a remote island off the west coast of Africa. He has been entered for the Worldwide Junior Extreme General Knowledge Competition this summer. He learnt to read when he was two,' he informed everybody.

Delilah groaned.

'He was almost as clever when he was two as I was when I was two,' said Mr Smart.

'I'm sure I could read when I was two, too,' said Mrs Smart.

'When you were too, too what?' demanded Mr Smart.

But Mrs Smart had stopped listening. She was checking her rather perfect profile in the shiny side of the toaster.

* * *

The next day, as soon as Mr and Mrs Smart had hurried off to the Big Brains Institute, Delilah started learning more general knowledge for the Worldwide Junior Extreme General Knowledge competition.

'I'm going to be busy all day,' she said wearily.

Granny Grabbers went and fetched a bucket and spade that she had found in the garden shed and brought some mud indoors and piled it on the cosy rug in front of the fire. She made a mud castle with mud towers and mud ramparts and other muddy features and she decorated it with bits of Mrs Smart's jewellery and some ornaments from the china cabinet. When it was finished, she and Sir Isaac Newton Bear sat in front of it and cooked crumpets on toasting forks.

However it was all no use.

Every time she went to try and persuade

Delilah to join in Delilah said no. She stayed in front of the computer all day. Her head hurt. But she wouldn't give up.

Granny Grabbers cleared all the mud away before Mr and Mrs Smart came home. She sat knitting three scarves at once in the utility room. She looked the same as ever, except her headlamps were a very dark blue, their saddest colour of all.

4

The Talking Granny

A few days after the whole miserable 'Babbatunde boy genius' business Delilah went to the corner shop, as usual, to get Mr Smart's Sunday paper.

She immediately met a very annoying little girl who was eating an ice cream by the door.

'Why are you always on your own?' said the little girl, staring up at her and licking the ice cream, which looked very yummy indeed.

'I live very nearby,' said Delilah. 'There is a cycle path and only one road to cross and it has buttons and a Green Man.' She wasn't alone anyway; she had Sir Isaac Newton in the basket on her bicycle. Only that morning he had told her that S was for septic, stomach and sick.

'I've got my granny,' said the little girl in an important voice.

Delilah looked around and there was a nice, friendly-looking woman holding some shopping bags.

'My granny's called Granny Brown and I've got another one at home called Granny Jones. She's my mummy's mummy,' said the little girl. 'You're always by yourself; you're weird.'

'I've got a granny at home too,' said Delilah firmly. 'And she's called Granny Grabbers. She hasn't come out because she's got lots of other things to do. She's recharging her batteries today.'

'That's what I need,' said the little girl's granny, laughing.

Delilah tried to smile. But she could hardly

think straight. She'd just had an idea. And it was huge.

When she and Sir Isaac got back to the house, Auntie Tillie had arrived for a visit. She was sitting at the kitchen table having a cup of tea with Mr Smart. Granny Grabbers was by the sink unpacking bags of vegetables with a lot of grabbers at once.

'Aren't you lonely?' Auntie Tillie asked Delilah in a quiet voice. 'You don't seem to have any friends.'

'Don't be silly, Tillie,' explained Mr Smart, full of good cheer. 'Friends would be a distraction. Delilah is busy learning things for the competition. Haven't you checked our website recently?'

Tillie rolled her eyes at Granny Grabbers, who rolled her headlamps in reply.

'I'm not lonely because I've got Granny Grabbers and Sir Isaac Newton,' said Delilah to Auntie Tillie. 'But I wish she could talk. I think maybe you can send off for an extra bit and add it to her circuits.'

'Don't be silly, Delilah,' said Mr Smart. 'There is absolutely no need for the childcare machine to talk. It would be expensive and unnecessary. Your mother and I are both jolly good at talking and you can listen to us whenever you want.'

Auntie Tillie glanced over at Granny Grabbers, who was peeling and washing carrots at the same time and splattering her front with water and carrot skin. Granny Grabbers shrugged some shoulders.

'By the way, Tillie,' said Mrs Smart, who had come tripping into the room. 'Thank you, but the present you've bought for Delilah wasn't very educational so I've put it in the garage with the others. She's not going to prepare for the competition by going up and down on a garden swing, now, is she?'

F is for Failure?

'I wish you *could* talk,' said Delilah to Granny Grabbers the next day. 'We could, you know, what's it called, *chat* and stuff.'

Granny Grabbers had broken another plate. They were sweeping up the pieces and hiding them in the dustbin. (She was very good at looking after Delilah and very bad at housework.)

'Look!' said Delilah suddenly, fishing around in the bin. 'Dad's been cleaning out his workshop again. These are from inside that radio he was trying to fix . . .' She waved a handful of wires and connections. 'And these are from the telly he was trying to fix, and these are from the computer . . .' She was holding a small speaker. 'And this is from that mobile phone he stood on, and then was trying to fix . . .'

Mr Smart, of course, was very, very clever. However, he was no good at fixing things because he always lost his temper.

'And I don't know what these are from,' added Delilah, finding yet more wires and circuits. 'But they *look* useful. I bet if I put all these inside you you'd be able to talk in no time. After all, radios and TVs can talk, can't they?' Granny Grabbers headlamps turned bright purple with alarm.

There wasn't much time because Mr and Mrs Smart would be home from work at any moment. Delilah whizzed about, clutching Sir Isaac Newton under one arm.

'D is for disaster, danger and doom,'

he muttered. Darkly.

Delilah fetched a screwdriver, a hammer and a hacksaw for taking things apart and a very small soldering iron for joining wires and circuits together.

Granny Grabbers stood next to her, twitching her grabbers in terror and standing on the hammer to hide it.

'I'll just unscrew this panel on your side,' said Delilah, trying to sound soothing, like a dentist. 'You shouldn't feel anything. Wave a grabber if it hurts.'

She didn't have a clue what to do. She quickly jammed all the bits inside Granny Grabbers and tried to join them to the wires and things that were there already using the very small soldering iron. (Don't try this at home; you will get electrocuted for sure.)

It was all very higgledy-piggledy.

They heard Mr and Mrs Smart's car stopping outside and Delilah fixed Granny Grabbers' panel back as quickly as possible and rushed off to put the tools away. When she got back Granny Grabbers was standing where she'd left her, not doing anything.

'Are you all right?' whispered Delilah.

Granny Grabbers nodded thoughtfully. She moved slowly off down the hall making a strange rattling noise and shut herself in the cupboard under the stairs.

'What on earth's been going on?' demanded Mr Smart. He had wandered into the kitchen without his shoes and stood on a lot of sharp bits of wire and screws and things on the floor.

'It's my fault, Dad,' said Delilah, wringing her hands. 'I was doing an experiment. I didn't have time to sweep up.'

'The childcare machine should sweep up,' grumbled Mr Smart. 'It is inefficient. I don't understand what it does all day.'

Delilah crept down the hall to the cupboard under the stairs.

'Are you all right?' she whispered to the outside of the door.

There was no answer.

By now Delilah was sure that the worst had happened.

She had broken Granny Grabbers.

She went and fetched Sir Isaac Newton. She sat down on the floor outside the cupboard and hugged him.

'F is for failure,' he wheezed. Mournfully.

6

Yummy Cardboard

Teatime came. Granny Grabbers was still not available.

'I expect it's doing the ironing,' said Mr Smart. 'It makes a terrible mess of it. I found a shirt the other day with a hole burnt right through it.'

'Well, never mind that now, dear,' began Mrs Smart.

'*And* it gets muddled. Yesterday I saw it empty the kitchen bin into the dishwasher—'

'Well, *never mind* that now,' repeated Mrs Smart, who was even more extremely pleased with herself than normal. 'I've got the most lovely surprise for Delilah.'

She put an enormous packet on the table.

'A special yummy new food has been invented just for children like you. High Protein Brain Food Biscuits to help your brain go faster. You don't have to eat anything else from now on. They have everything you need in them. They'll help you with all the things we want you to do, not just the competition, although of course that's terribly important, but things like music, ballet, ice-skating, tap-dancing, rock-climbing . . .' She trailed off, a dreamy expression on her face as she imagined Delilah being very, very good at everything in the world.

Delilah stared at the box in horror. It looked like dog food.

'They come in three super flavours, darling: strawberry, sardine and spinach. Which would you like to try first?'

Delilah tried a bit of the strawberry.

It was very hard and pink and tasted like cardboard. She tried a bit of the sardine. It tasted like salty cardboard.

Finally she tried the spinach. It tasted like the strawberry but was green instead of pink.

'They're all horrible,' she said miserably.

'Oh dear, never mind,' said Mrs Smart, having a big mouthful of mint choc chip ice cream. 'You want to win the competition, don't you? Think of that Babbatunde. I expect he eats them all the time.'

'Why don't you two have some?' asked Delilah.

Mr Smart helped himself to more chocolate sauce. 'Your mother and I are as clever as it is possible for us to be,' he said with his mouth full.

Delilah chewed the corner of her strawberry Brain Food Biscuit.

(She didn't know it yet but far away on the

island of Amania, Babbatunde the Boy Genius was at that very moment secretly burying his Brain Food Biscuits under a mango tree in the moonlight. He didn't like them either. In fact, everyone in the whole world thought they were disgusting, including the people who invented them.)

Still no news from the cupboard under the stairs.

Bedtime came.

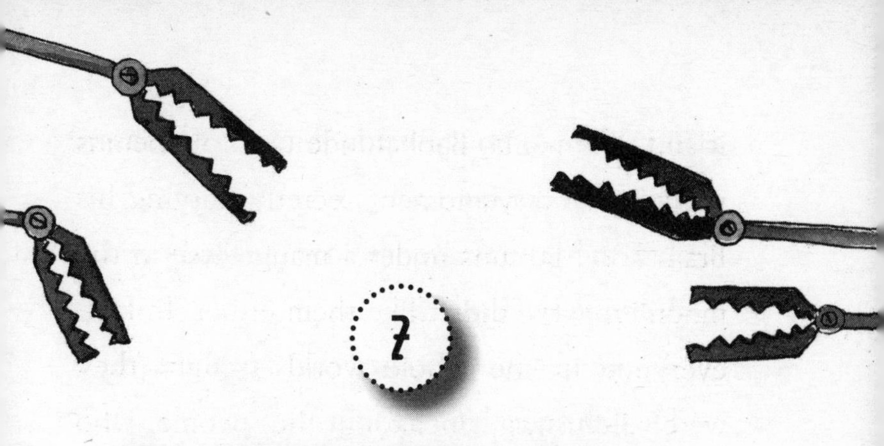

7

The Night-Time Visitor

Very, very miserable now, Delilah put herself to bed. She snuggled up beside Sir Isaac.

'M is for mistake,' he informed her, 'misery and murder.'

'Oh, shut UP!' yelled Delilah. 'Don't you know *any* nice words?' And she threw him across the room and he hit the door with quite a bang and didn't say anything at all.

This was too much.

She had broken Granny Grabbers and now she had broken Sir Isaac.

Delilah climbed out of the bed and crept

across the room towards him. His glasses crunched under her foot.

Just then the bedroom door creaked open.

Very, very slowly.

A strange figure loomed there in the dark.

Delilah squealed in fright.

There was a click.

The strange figure had turned on the light. It was Granny Grabbers wearing a blue beret with two shiny black plaits attached to it, and holding two grabbers behind her back.

Delilah flung her arms around her.

'Oh, thank goodness! I've been so worried! Oh, Granny Grabbers, I love you so much! And I promise I'll never try to make you talk again!'

Granny Grabbers hugged Delilah.

'Why are you wearing that hat thing?' whispered Delilah. 'Did you get it out of Mum and Dad's costume box?'

(Mr and Mrs Smart had been in a lot of pantomimes since they had starred as the Ugly

Sisters and they kept a big box full of costumes in the spare bedroom.)

Granny Grabbers nodded.

'What are you hiding behind your back?' whispered Delilah.

Granny Grabbers straightened her beret and plaits, which had slipped forward over her headlamps during all the hugging. She rolled into the bedroom and shut the door. Her headlamps glowed red with glee and excitement.

Then, with a triumphant swing of a grabber from behind her back, she waved a great big chocolate cake under Delilah's nose. It had three layers and almost completely filled one of the very special serving plates the Smarts used for their very special dinner parties.

As soon as she saw the cake, which was buried in thick delicious-looking icing, Delilah realized that she was terribly hungry and she began cramming big sticky bits into her mouth.

'This is really, really yummy. I didn't know you could cook anything like this,' she began with her mouth full, getting icing on her face.

Then she remembered Sir Isaac and stopped in the middle of a big chomp.

'Oh no, Granny Grabbers, something terrible's happened to Sir Isaac Newton. I – well, I sort of dropped him in a sort of, well, throwing sort of way.'

Granny Grabbers turned her headlamps towards Sir Isaac. He was lying on his back on the floor.

She picked him up, and his glasses, and tucked him under one of her many armpits. She straightened her beret again.

Once more Delilah stopped frantically eating chocolate cake.

She had a sudden feeling that something extraordinary was going to happen.

And then it did.

'Good evenings. We must protect the planet

and the wildy animals,' a warm, husky voice announced. 'In tonight's episode of Vettydocs in Action we will repair and upgrade this bear.'

The voice was coming from Granny Grabbers.

'You're talking,' spluttered Delilah, showering crumbs everywhere. 'Have you turned into a radio?'

She took two steps backwards and sat down on the bed unexpectedly.

Granny Grabbers waved some anxious grabbers. She rolled forward.

Delilah jumped across the bed holding up a pillow in front of her. All this talking was pretty scary.

'Important news flash . . . Grabbers is not computer, television, telephone or radio,' said Granny Grabbers firmly. 'Or anything else. Except Grabbers.'

Delilah stared at her.

'Child unit must not be worrisome and

ditheridoo,' added Granny Grabbers. 'Grabberspeak is better than no speak.'

'Oh, yes,' exclaimed Delilah. 'I didn't mean—'

'Then let us boogie on down. And it is big good nightie and pyjamas to all our listeners. Good nightie and nice dream. We will be on the air in the kitchen at seven o'clock tomorrow morning.' She trundled to the door, looked back over her shoulders and added, 'Fasten your seat belts.'

Then she closed the door quietly behind her.

Delilah heard her humming a little tune as she went out. Then the familiar boing, boing, boing as she went down the stairs.

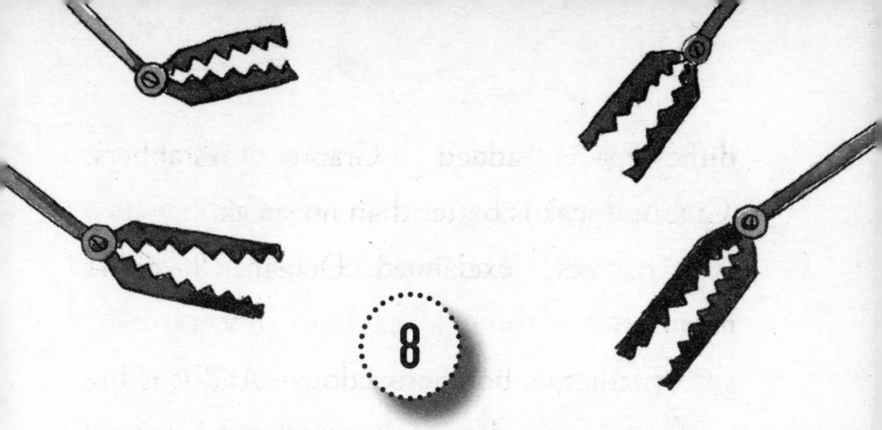

8

The Relaxing Tomatoes and the Old Friend

Next morning Delilah jumped out of bed, stepped in the chocolate cake and rushed down to the kitchen.

There was Granny Grabbers crashing about at the sink. She had clearly had a good rummage through Mr and Mrs Smart's pantomime costume box. She was wearing a pale-yellow hat with long yellow rabbit ears, a pearl necklace and a curly moustache.

The dreaded Brain Food box stood importantly in the middle of the table with a bowl of green biscuits and a glass of water.

'Good mornings,' said Granny Grabbers in a cheery voice. 'The modern woman likes to express herself through her choice of accessories,' she added, pointing at the bunny ears.

'I'm not sure about the moustache,' hissed Delilah.

Granny Grabbers pulled the moustache off her face and stuck it on her front instead.

'Experts suggest five potions of fruit and vegetables every day,' she announced. 'A good breakfast boils the energy. Always clean your teeths.'

'Delilah!' called Mrs Smart from upstairs. 'Remember to only eat Brain Food. I left it out for you last night.'

Granny Grabbers seized the bowl, tipped the Brain Food Biscuits into the compost-recycling bin and poured potato peelings on top.

She shoved another bowl into Delilah's

hands. It was full of cereal with bits of raspberry, banana, nuts and raisins.

'This morning in the greenhouse with gardener Grabbers,' she said.

'What?' exclaimed Delilah.

'Get away from stress. Plants are relaxing. Lavender is a blue dilly dilly. Tomatoes are red.'

Footsteps on the stairs.

'Remember, you don't need any other food, Delilah darling. It would just slow down your digestion and brain development,' called Mrs Smart sweetly.

Granny Grabbers opened the door to the utility room and pushed Delilah straight through and out into the garden.

So Delilah had her breakfast in the greenhouse, among the red and relaxing tomatoes. And Hercules the cat came and sat with her, because he liked relaxing too.

As soon as she had seen her parents rushing

off to work, Delilah took her empty bowl back into the kitchen.

Granny Grabbers had finished clearing up the breakfast things. There was a broken cup on the draining board.

Delilah found her in the little room known as the study. She was busy at the computer.

'What are you doing?' whispered Delilah.

She didn't remember seeing Granny Grabbers using the computer before. Then she spotted one of Mrs Smart's credit cards clutched firmly in a nearby grabber.

Granny Grabbers was examining the internet. Apparently she had already visited itzyditzyrobotbitzy.com and now she was gazing at gerbilsmakesense.com.

'Granny Grabbers,' whispered Delilah. 'Are you sure this is a good idea?'

'The little petlings are an important part of childhood,' said Granny Grabbers, not taking her headlamps off the screen.

'You're not using Mum's credit cards, are you?'

Granny Grabbers was tapping out numbers on the keyboard. Several more cards were stacked neatly on the desk.

'You're not, are you?' repeated Delilah.

'The person you are calling is busy. Please try again later beep,' said Granny Grabbers.

Delilah gave up. She stared at the screen. There was no doubt about it. Granny Grabbers was buying a gerbil.

After that, for several mornings running, interesting parcels kept arriving at the front door after Mr and Mrs Smart had gone to work.

Delilah was in the greenhouse having breakfast as usual when she saw a white envelope stuck in among the branches of one of the tomato plants.

It had 'Delilah' written on it in big, wobbly letters.

She opened it and found a card inside, undoubtedly written by grabber.

we have big pleasure to inviting you to
cupboard under the stairs.
catch up with an old friend.
there's no bear like an old bear.

Delilah set off for the hall. Mr and Mrs Smart hadn't realized it but the cupboard under the stairs had become Granny Grabbers' private place.

She opened the door slowly.

Everything looked very dark and dusty and small. There were the brooms. There was the ancient vacuum cleaner.

Then, suddenly, a light came on. The back of the cupboard swung open. Delilah couldn't

THE DENTISTS OF DOOM
Box Of Bits

believe her eyes. There was a cosy secret room reaching right under the stairs. Granny Grabbers must have rigged up some electricity. A green lava lamp glowed in the corner. Pictures of the famous rock band The Dentists of Doom were pinned to the wall. There was a framed photograph of Delilah, and a workbench made out of planks, which Delilah had last seen in the garage.

And there was Sir Isaac Newton, sitting up, his glasses mended and a new striped bow tie around his neck.

Delilah gave a yell of delight, picked him up and hugged him tightly.

'C is for cuddle, L is for love,' he said in a muffled voice.

9

The Back End of a Horse

That night, when Mr and Mrs Smart came home, everything was perfect and calm.

Delilah had done the ironing. She hoped that Mr Smart would stop complaining about Granny Grabbers if he didn't have quite so many holes in his shirts. Now she was upstairs studying.

'Why is the childcare machine wearing a hat again?' asked Mr Smart.

Granny Grabbers was wearing a baseball cap perched on the top of her head and held in place with sticky tape. (Her head was too big for her to wear it any other way.) She was polishing the table in the hall.

'Oh, I expect it's just a game Delilah has been playing,' said Mrs Smart. 'She gets things out of our pantomime box. I hope we're in another one this year, darling. Last Christmas the director said I was born for my role.'

'That was definitely when you were the back end of the horse,' said Mr Smart, who was trying and failing to mend the hairdryer.

'I was NOT. I have NEVER been ANY PART of a horse, AS YOU WELL KNOW. I was the WICKED WITCH. You're just jealous, darling, because you were only Man-in-Market-when-Puss-in-Boots-was-Doing-his-Shopping. Hardly a very important part. Even then you messed it up by standing on Puss's tail.'

At this point Granny Grabbers came bustling into the room with a basket of dusters and polish and things dangling from one grabber and Sir Isaac Newton dangling from another.

'Oh, how sweet,' exclaimed Mrs Smart. 'Delilah must have made a sweet little tie for her Brain Building Bear.'

'But that looks like my new silk tie for special work meetings,' protested Mr Smart. 'Someone has cut it up!'

'Oh, don't make such a *fuss*, darling,' trilled Mrs Smart as Granny Grabbers tried to get past her, aiming for the kitchen. 'Look, in its simple, humble way, the robot is trying to show me what Delilah has done.'

Granny Grabbers came to a halt. In her simple, humble way, she held out Sir Isaac and gently squeezed him around the middle. Her headlamps had turned very slightly green.

'I is for irritating, imbecile and idiot,' hissed Sir Isaac. Fortunately at that very moment Mr Smart pressed something on the hairdryer and it made an ear-splitting whistling noise, causing everyone present, including Mrs Smart, to quickly block their auditory detectors.

10

And Now the Weather Forecast

Auntie Tillie lived a long way away but it didn't stop her from turning up several times a year to see Delilah, and embarrassing Mr and Mrs Smart by parking her scruffy van outside their house.

She turned up in this manner a few weeks after Granny Grabbers began to Grabberspeak.

Most unusually, Mrs Smart rushed out of the front door to greet her.

'We've got the most exciting news. We've enrolled Delilah at Madame Delightful's Dance

Academy on Thursday evenings. And we're considering Introductory Sumo Wrestling for her on Fridays. But the really wonderful thing is that the Worldwide Junior Extreme General Knowledge Competition is really soon and we are sure she's going to win.'

Auntie Tillie dropped her rucksack on the floor with a thud.

Granny Grabbers, vacuuming the hall, waved nicely and then somehow got the vacuum cleaner stuck on one of her wheels and had to be rescued by Delilah.

'I was going to ask if I could take her to the park and swings and slides and feed the ducks and eat ice cream,' said Tillie. She always asked but it never happened.

Delilah could guess exactly what Mrs Smart was going to say.

'Delilah doesn't eat ice cream,' said Mrs Smart. 'She only has special Brain Food. And now she doesn't have time to go anywhere. She has to study. She's ever so keen. We don't have to push her, you know. She pushes herself.'

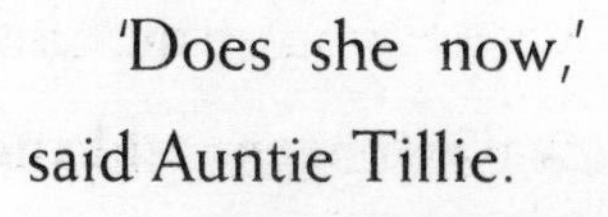

'Does she now,' said Auntie Tillie.

Delilah could have sworn that Granny Grabbers made a rude gesture. But at that moment Mrs Smart turned round and Granny Grabbers raised her hat instead. It was a very large straw one with corks hanging on bits of string all around the brim.

'Granny Grabbers really, really likes hats and costumes and things,' explained Delilah, as soon as her parents had gone to do their exercises.

'I can see that,' said Auntie Tillie.

'She found some in a box,' added Delilah. 'Then she ordered some more on the internet.'

'Oh,' said Auntie Tillie.

They were in the utility room. A gerbil peered at them from inside an exceptionally large cage.

'That's Dr Doomy,' explained Delilah. 'He's named after Granny Grabbers' favourite rock band. Except they're dentists. The Dentists of Doom. Pets are an important part of childhood. And Granny Grabbers can talk now. She speaks Grabberspeak.'

Just then, Granny Grabbers opened the door from the garden and bumbled in carrying a big wicker basket and a lot of clothes pegs.

'In our hectic modern world it is important for children to have contact with nice auntie people,' she told Auntie Tillie shyly.

Auntie Tillie grinned.

'Delilah has provided speech. I am whizz bang. Gerbils are vegetarian,' added Granny Grabbers.

'This Dr Doomy is a great idea,' said Auntie Tillie. 'Delilah needs things like that. You look after her very well.'

Granny Grabbers' headlamp lids fluttered with pride. Her headlamps flashed red and she dropped all the clothes pegs.

'Do your mum and dad know about the Grabberspeak?' asked Tillie as they scrabbled about on the floor to pick them up. (Granny Grabbers extended her arms in these situations, being unable to bend in the middle.)

'No, of course not,' exclaimed Delilah. 'And I'm so worried about this competition. If I don't win they'll never get over it.'

Auntie Tillie sighed.

'I've got a present for you,' she said. 'Your mum's checking it now to see if it's suitable.'

She had never given up bringing Delilah presents. Even though every single one she had ever brought was still in the garage in its box.

However, this time Tillie's present had passed the test. Mrs Smart called out that Delilah could come and see it, and Delilah ran through to the hall, very excited.

'It's a globe that lights up,' Auntie Tillie told Granny Grabbers.

Granny Grabbers nodded.

'This competition sounds like the last straw to me,' added Tillie.

'And now the weather forecast,' said Granny Grabbers. 'Storms, rain and misery in all areas. High pressure on everyone.' Her headlamps turned a deep and sorrowful blue.

'You've said it, Granny G,' said Auntie Tillie.

11

Trolley Rage

'The Worldwide Junior Extreme General Knowledge Competition is starting in two weeks, two days, three hours and six point six minutes,' said Mr Smart a few days later. 'It is very important that you don't let the Smart family down.'

Delilah was sitting at the kitchen table. She was trying to remember all the capital cities of the world. She was so worried about the competition it was making her ill.

Sir Isaac Newton was on her knee.

'Don't you think you're a bit old to be

carrying that bear everywhere?' said Mrs Smart. She wanted everyone to think that Delilah was the most grown-up child in the competition as well as the cleverest.

Delilah didn't reply. She hugged Sir Isaac tightly. 'S is for shut your stupid face,' he whispered.

Fortunately only Delilah heard him. The dishwasher had started to make a loud wailing noise.

'It's going wrong again,' yelled Mr Smart. And he jumped up, rushed over and began thumping all the buttons on the front.

Granny Grabbers sailed in from the living room where she had been dusting. She was holding two feather dusters and a jug of water for watering the plants. She was using two more grabbers to block her auditory detectors.

She reached politely past Mr Smart with her one spare grabber and tapped the dishwasher gently on the side.

The wailing stopped.

'I think the childcare robot is cleverer than you, darling,' laughed Mrs Smart.

'Nonsense,' snapped Mr Smart. He was trying to push past Granny Grabbers, which was not only rude but impossible. He looked very cross.

'Do you realize,' he spat, 'that this great clumsy robot is so out of date they don't even make it any more? OUCH!'

Granny Grabbers, by some strange accident, had got one of her grabbers tangled in his hair.

'Oh, do keep still, darling,' cried Mrs Smart laughing. 'It's trying to untangle itself.'

Granny Grabbers had delicately freed her grabber. She rolled quietly out of the way.

'I was looking at the Happy Home Robotics website,' continued Mr Smart, rubbing his head. 'The latest model is coming out just before Christmas. It's called the Nanny Deluxe. It's not only much more *efficient*, it is much *better-looking*.'

'I think I'll go up to my room,' said Delilah in a small voice. If they really decided to replace Granny Grabbers it would be the absolute end of the world and life would not be worth living.

But Mrs Smart wanted to test her on capital cities. Delilah got the first ten right. Then she got three wrong in a row.

Silence fell in the kitchen.

Granny Grabbers was standing tidily in a corner, hiding a clump of Mr Smart's hair behind her back. She clenched a number of grabbers.

'No, no, NO!' exclaimed Mr Smart, who was now in a terrible mood. 'Our family do NOT get things wrong, Delilah. You must study harder. Coming second is simply not good enough!'

Delilah sniffed. She tried not to start crying but she just couldn't help it. Big tears began to trickle down her face.

Granny Grabbers' headlamps flashed their

most angry and terrible lime green. Very quickly, and much less clumsily than normal, she picked up the jug of water for watering the houseplants and threw it over Mr Smart.

Delilah squeezed her eyes shut.

'This robot is MALFUNCTIONING!' yelled Mr Smart, dripping water everywhere.

Mrs Smart was laughing so much, she almost fell off her chair.

'I'VE HAD ENOUGH!' shouted Mr Smart. 'As soon as we get back from the competition I'm getting rid of it! It's old, it's ugly, it makes too many mistakes, it's got a ridiculous number of arms and it's going to the TIP!' He stormed out of the room and squelched up the stairs to get changed.

'He's quite right, Delilah,' said Mrs Smart, wiping her eyes after all her merriment. 'Last time we had a dinner party I had to ask it to keep out of sight. I don't want my friends to think I can't afford a new one.'

Delilah snatched up her books and papers and Sir Isaac Newton and rushed out of the house. Granny Grabbers followed her, rocking and rattling, and they skidded into the greenhouse, knocking over the tomato plants. Hercules shot out in a blur of panic and claws.

'We apologize to all our listeners! Self-control circuits overridden by trolley rage!' gabbled Granny Grabbers, waving and blinking and flashing her headlamps all different colours.

'You're not a trolley!' cried Delilah.

'We apologize we apolly apolly a polly parrot a parrot a carrot steam the vegetables eatables eaty tables fresh fruit vitamins child needs love affection fresh air fresh fish oily boily fishy wishy on a little dishy—'

'STOP!' begged Delilah desperately. She tried to hug Granny Grabbers but Granny Grabbers was waving her grabbers much too fast.

'Old models to be scrapped, insides

removed, body made into dustbin, grabbers into deskylamps, who will protect and guard child unit? Sunblock, always clean teeths, vitamins, too much pressure to succeed, grannies to be scrapped, who will provide component of wisdom? Who will complete circuits of love?'

'GRANNY!' cried Delilah. 'IT'S ALL RIGHT! DON'T WORRY!'

But it wasn't all right. And they both knew it.

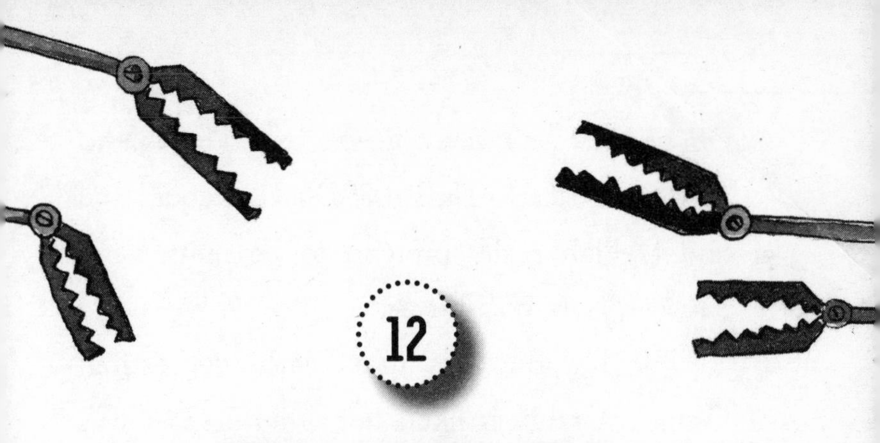

12

Observe the Ant

That night Delilah couldn't sleep.

After a while she crept downstairs, carrying Sir Isaac Newton and, out of habit, her spelling book. (Waterproof, for bathtime fun.)

Granny Grabbers was in the utility room next to Dr Doomy. The shock of Mr Smart's announcement about the tip had worn off. Now she was calm and stern and determined. She had plugged herself into the wall to recharge her batteries and was reading a number of books at once, all to do with escaping. They included *The Highway Code* and *Teach yourself to*

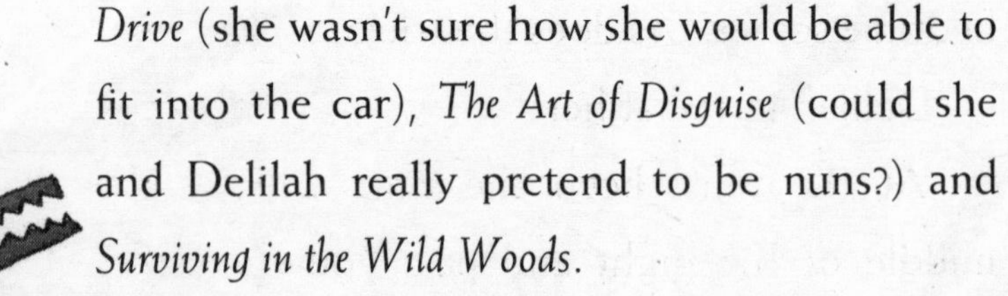

Drive (she wasn't sure how she would be able to fit into the car), *The Art of Disguise* (could she and Delilah really pretend to be nuns?) and *Surviving in the Wild Woods*.

The last one was particularly depressing. Granny Grabbers liked her comforts. At this very moment, for example, she was wearing a cosy blue nightcap and three pairs of matching blue fluffy bedsocks on her grabbers.

In addition to all this she was using her headphones, which were clamped over her auditory detectors. The sinister howls, wails and bangs of The Dentists of Doom leaked into the utility room.

Delilah pattered in and Granny Grabbers turned off the Dentists and took the headphones off.

'Are you having the problems sleeping?' she asked Delilah. 'Lines are open. Doctor Grabbers is here to help. Children need at least ten hours' sleep a night. A warm drink at bedtime sometimes does the trick . . .'

Delilah stared at her.

'At the third beep the time will be the middle of the night and past your bedtime,' added Granny Grabbers rather sternly. 'Beep, beep, beep—'

'I'm so scared,' whispered Delilah. 'I'm so scared he'll send you to the tip. I don't know what I'd do, I don't know what—'

Granny Grabbers hugged her with all six grabbers at once. Further speech was impossible for a moment.

'Child unit must sleep to rest brain and build strength,' said Granny Grabbers eventually. 'Grabbers makes electric think through hours of darkness. *The Highway Code* is book of wisdom. Nuns have habits. Observe behaviour of wildlife. Bees lead to honey. Rubby the little sticks to make fire.'

'What?' said Delilah.

'We now join our listeners in moment of

calm to endy evening. Winds light to moderate. Rain in some areas will give way to sun in morning.'

As sometimes happened, Delilah didn't really understand the words. It didn't matter though, because she understood the meaning. Granny Grabbers was going to have an idea and it was possible that, somehow, everything was going to be all right.

Granny Grabbers unplugged herself and removed her nightclothes. Then she fetched Auntie Tillie's present, which Mrs Smart had put tidily back into its box.

There was a tremendous burst of tearing and whirling grabbers and tiny bits of cardboard settled on the floor like snow. This was how she always unpacked things. She shredded the box.

It was a very large, very beautiful globe. Auntie Tillie had saved up for a whole year to buy it.

Delilah switched it on and all the seas and oceans of the world were deep blue and twinkling with waves. The North Pole and the South Pole were bright with snow. The mountains and the plains, the forests and the cities were brown and green and silver and gold.

Granny Grabbers and Delilah gazed at it together.

'I'll never be clever enough for Mum and

Dad,' whispered Delilah. 'Even if I win this competition there will always be another one.'

She pointed at a tiny island.

'I bet no one lives there,' she said wistfully. 'If we went there – you and me and Sir Isaac and Dr Doomy – nobody could take you to the tip. And we wouldn't have to worry about Brain Food, or competitions, ever again.'

There was a pause and then a whirring noise. A sure sign that Granny Grabbers was going to say something important.

'Do-it-yourself,' she said. 'Even the most difficult jobs can be whizz-bang success with the right planning, the right tools and the right brothers.'

Delilah frowned. 'The right brothers?'

'Big achievements made out of very many little steps. Observe the ant,' added Granny Grabbers.

Delilah looked at her. Then, very puzzled, she went to bed.

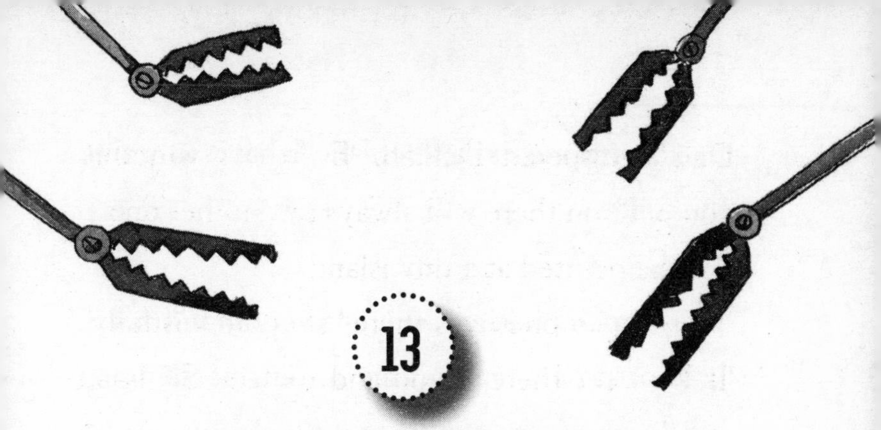

13

Could your Dog Play the Piano?

It was a long way to the city where the Worldwide Junior Extreme General Knowledge Competition was to be held. On the train Mrs Smart kept talking to the other passengers.

'Where are you going?' she asked everyone who was sitting anywhere near them. And then, without waiting for a reply, 'We're off to the Worldwide Junior Extreme General Knowledge Competition sponsored by Brain Food Inc. Our daughter is very likely to win. You might want her autograph.'

'Excuse me,' said Delilah. 'I have to go to the toilet.'

They arrived late at night at a very grand hotel. Lots of taxis were pulling up outside bringing families from the station and the airport.

There was a revolving door into the hotel, which Delilah knew that Granny Grabbers would have liked. Then they rode up and up in a lift full of mirrors. Delilah was sure that Granny Grabbers would have liked that too.

But Granny Grabbers was back at home, and had waved goodbye to her through the kitchen window.

'Do try to look more cheerful, dear. This is the most fun, exciting, fab, cool thing you've ever done,' said Mrs Smart as she unpacked the five new outfits she had bought herself for the trip.

'This takes me back to when I was your age,' said Mr Smart. 'I loved competitions. I won a year's supply of dog food in a spelling competition. My parents bought a dog straight away. Of course, he turned out to be very talented. He could play the piano, if I remember rightly.'

Mrs Smart frowned. '*Could* your dog play the piano, darling? Are you quite sure? Aren't you confusing it with our cat, who could do headstands and was in the *Amazing Book of Records*?'

Delilah wandered over to the window and looked out. Granny Grabbers would definitely have liked all those lights. It was really, really strange not having her there.

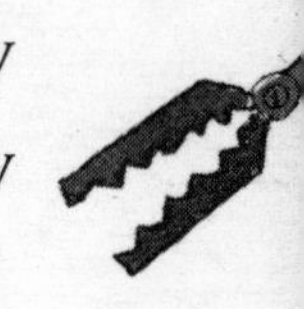

14

Best Wishes from Dr Doomy

The next morning everyone went down to breakfast in the dining room. Brain Food Biscuits were piled on every table.

A man with a big Brain Food Inc. badge went from table to table, smiling and nodding.

'Ah, the Smart family, and you must be Delilah. We are very pleased you made the trip. I'm sure you're going to enjoy yourself. We've got some really famous children here; Babbatunde arrived last night from Amania. What do you think of the hotel, Delilah? Is it

SMART enough for you?'

The Smart family stared at him in silence.

'What a cute bear,' he said hurriedly, making the mistake of prodding Sir Isaac Newton playfully in the chest.

Sir Isaac's glasses glinted. 'R is for R you as dumb as you look?' he growled. The man gulped as if he were swallowing a Brain Food Biscuit himself. Then he rushed off to greet the people at the next table.

'Darling,' began Mrs Smart doubtfully, 'did that bear just say—'

'LADIES AND GENTLEMEN, PARENTS, GUARDIANS AND CONTESTANTS,' boomed a voice coming out of a loudspeaker. 'Please attend the make-up room and then join us in the ballroom where the children will have a super fun day answering questions and doing puzzles. All events will be filmed for television.'

'Oh, lovely!' squeaked Mrs Smart. 'I think we

should be made up too, don't you, darling? In case the camera picks us out of the audience.'

Delilah pushed her uneaten Brain Food Biscuit round her plate. If only she was at home with Granny Grabbers eating her secret scrambled eggs. How was Granny Grabbers? What hat was she wearing today?

But there was no escape.

Off she went to make-up.

Then the competition began.

At lunchtime they stopped for a break. Brain Food Soup, Brain Food Burgers and Brain Food Sandwiches were available in the dining room.

'I wonder where Babbatunde is,' said Mr Smart, who was wrapping some burger in his handkerchief to throw away later.

'He's in a different group to me,' explained Delilah. 'I'll only meet him if we're the last two left.'

'Oh, DO try to look more cheerful, Delilah,' exclaimed Mr Smart, putting on a big toothy smile himself. 'That camera is pointing right at us. I think they know that I was "Little Mr Brain Cells" when I was seven.'

Delilah sneaked away, with Sir Isaac under her arm.

Then, horrors, the bouncing man with the Brain Food Inc. badge came bouncing up to her.

'You're Delilah Smart, aren't you?' he asked, eyeing Sir Isaac nervously.

'Yes,' said Delilah, her heart sinking.

'Parcel for you at reception. Came by post,' said the man, and bounced hurriedly away again.

Delilah dived across the crowded room and down the wide corridor towards the front door. For a few wild and wonderful moments she thought that Granny Grabbers might have wrapped herself up and posted herself to the hotel.

But the parcel wasn't big enough.

Although it *was* quite big.

And fairly heavy.

Delilah took it up to the bedroom and unwrapped it in the ensuite bathroom.

A very large amount of brown sticky tape – probably a whole roll – had been wound round and round it at crazy angles. And the spiky writing on the outside was grabberwriting.

Layer after layer of paper lay on the floor of the bathroom. At last Delilah reached a tin box in the middle of all the wrapping. It was a bit dirty on the outside and she thought she recognized it from the garage at home. However, inside it was all clean. It contained packets of nuts, dried fruit, hard-boiled eggs, a large chocolate cake and a tomato.

And there was a message.

all well heres. very much sewing and hammering. dr doom sends best wishes. orville nearly ready. broke a plate yesterday. clean teeths.

love G.G.

Sewing? Hammering? What on earth was she going on about? And who was Orville? This name seemed a bit familiar to Delilah but she couldn't work out where she had heard it before. Perhaps Orville was another gerbil.

She ate several things out of the tin. Then she hid the message in her pocket and the cake tin under the bed.

Over the next two days she read the message again and again. It didn't make sense but that didn't matter. At least it was from Granny Grabbers.

15

Greetings, Earthlings

At last the competition was nearly over and there were only two children left.

One of them was Babbatunde, the Boy Genius from Amania.

The other was Delilah.

The final was to be in the morning.

The hotel was buzzing with excitement. Extra television cameras had arrived from fifteen different countries. The bouncy man from Brain Food Inc. practically flew along the corridors giving away T-shirts, china biscuit barrels and samples of disgusting Brain Biscuits.

It was announced that Brain Food Inc. would be launching a special new flavour of biscuit and naming it after the winner. (The new flavour, they explained, was impossible to describe. Which was not a surprise.)

'We'll go out this evening and let you do some studying,' said Delilah's mother. 'Remember, tomorrow is one of the most important days of my life.'

'And mine,' said Mr Smart, putting a bit more stuff on his hair.

'I know,' said Delilah. She was so used to feeling sick, she didn't even notice any more.

As soon as they had gone she locked up the bedroom and went downstairs with Sir Isaac. She had seen a public telephone near the front desk in its own tiny red-carpeted room. None of the children had been allowed to keep their mobiles, in case they used them to cheat.

She phoned home. She thought that if she

didn't hear Granny Grabbers' voice soon she would go mad.

Of course, no one except Delilah and Auntie Tillie knew that Granny Grabbers could speak. She never normally answered the phone.

Delilah let it ring three times, hung up and dialled again. This was the code they had arranged between them so Granny Grabbers would know to pick up.

'And a very good evenings to all our listeners at home and abroad,' said someone, sounding as if they had a bucket on their head.

'What's going on?' whispered Delilah. 'Who's Orville?'

There was a crash, then the unmistakable creaking of a grabber picking something up. 'We are apologetic for the interference,' said Granny Grabbers after a moment. 'Greetings, earthlings, we come in pieces.'

'What is going on?' whispered Delilah.

'I'm very pleased you asked me that

question,' said Granny Grabbers, suddenly sounding like a prime minister doing an interview on the news. 'All targets have been met. We are very, very happy with the way the project is going.'

'*What* project?' exclaimed Delilah.

There was another crash and then a buzzing noise.

And then just the dialling tone . . .

16

P is for Penthouse

Delilah almost dropped Sir Isaac. She tried to ring Granny Grabbers again but she didn't have enough change. She was so fed up she just about fell out of the stupid phone booth. Several children were standing around with their suitcases waiting for taxis. They were going home because they'd been eliminated from the competition. They recognized Delilah and laughed.

She marched to the lift but it had just left.

Then, because the children were still staring at her, she marched over to another, much smaller lift nearby.

'PRIVATE' it said on the shiny door. 'PENTHOUSE ONLY'. She reached to press the call lift button. But there wasn't a call lift button. Instead there was a little keypad with the numbers 1–9.

The children who were leaving watched her, sniggering. They were not friendly people.

One of them shouted, 'Hey, Smartie, how's your ickle teddy bear?' Delilah broke out in a sweat and started trying random numbers on the keypad.

'Can't oo pwess the wight button then, Smartie? I thought you were supposed to be so clever.'

Suddenly Delilah had an idea. It was the hotel phone number. Granny Grabbers had insisted on learning it by heart and had kept reciting it in the greenhouse.

Delilah punched it into the keypad.

The doors opened. She stepped inside and

they slid silently and expensively closed behind her. Then the lift began to move up.

Faster and faster.

A silky voice said, 'Penthouse: enjoy your stay,' and it stopped again and the door opened. Delilah, clutching Sir Isaac, stepped out into an extremely grand hallway with gold carpets and twinkling glass lights.

A boy in green striped robes was standing there holding a suitcase and a coat.

'Babbatunde?' said Delilah.

'Delilah?' said Babbatunde.

'What are you doing?' they both said at once.

'You're so smart, you tell me!' snapped Babbatunde.

'You work it out, Mr MegaBrain,' hissed Delilah.

'But this is the penthouse suite. Only

VIPs stay here. The lift has a security code,' said Babbatunde.

'I worked it out,' said Delilah airily. 'Although I think I was a bit lucky. Why are you carrying a suitcase and holding your coat? Are you going somewhere?'

Babbatunde looked quickly over his shoulder down the long golden hallway. There was the sound of voices and a door closing somewhere close by.

'Well?' said Delilah.

'Babbatunde! Come and do your human calculator practice!' called someone in a bossy manner.

'Excuse me, excuse me,' gabbled Babbatunde, suddenly pushing past Delilah into the lift and banging into Sir Isaac.

'G is for genius . . . NOT,' whispered Sir Isaac.

'What's going on?' yelped Delilah.

'Close the door! Go up! Go up!' cried

Babbatunde, lunging frantically at the buttons. More voices from the corridor.

The doors slid closed.

'Thanks,' said Babbatunde.

The lift was going up.

'Wouldn't it be more sensible to go down?' remarked Delilah coldly.

'I'm going up to my father's private helicopter. On the roof.'

Delilah was impressed, but didn't show it.

And a moment later they were on the roof with the lights of the city twinkling all around them.

'Thanks,' shouted Babbatunde again, over his shoulder this time. He was striding off towards the helipad. 'Enjoy the prize money, the international acclaim and the ten-year supply of vomit biscuits.'

Delilah couldn't believe what was happening. She ran to keep up with him.

'But where are you going?'

'It's obvious, isn't it? I'm running away. I can't cope if I don't win. My mother won't speak to me for a year. My father won't ever say how disappointed he is – but I will know. Plus our whole island is watching on TV. There's a public holiday specially. It'll be a national disaster.'

He switched on the engine.

'But you *will* win,' shouted Delilah above the noise. 'You're much cleverer than me.'

'Don't think so. Anyway. Can't cope if I *do* win,' he shouted back, pulling switches and pushing buttons. 'I never wanted to be famous and I don't want to be on TV. I hate all the fuss and the cameras and those biscuits made of dried animal dung. I'm fed up with the whole thing.'

The helicopter propellers began to turn. Delilah was blasted with noise and wind. Some sort of alarm was going off in there as well. Suddenly she had an absolutely wild and brilliant idea. It was very simple . . .

'Stop!' she yelled. 'I'm coming with you!'

She leapt into the passenger seat and pulled the door shut as they lurched into the air. Now people were running towards them across the roof, waving and shouting.

'My chess tutor, my memory tutor and the man who cooks my Brain Food,' explained Babbatunde breathlessly. 'And a couple of my bodyguards – lots of muscles but they can't run very fast.'

'Have you ever flown one of these before?' asked Delilah, trying to find the seat belts.

'I watched my dad once. Could you turn that dial a bit round to the left, please. I can't reach it.'

'You just *watched* him *once*?!'

They were flying now. The helipad, the people waving and shouting, and the hotel itself swung away behind them, getting smaller and smaller. Babbatunde leant back in his seat and grinned at her.

'Yeah,' he said. 'Only once. And then he let me have some lessons.'

Delilah did up Sir Isaac's safety harness, rather tightly.

'P is for parachute,' he said. Hopefully.

'That is some bear,' said Babbatunde.

They spun along in silence for a little while, only losing height and going sideways once, when Babbatunde looked under the seat to see if there was anything to eat.

'So where are we going?' asked Delilah.

'Anywhere you like,' he said, with his mouth full of stale crisps.

17

Orville

Back at the Smart family home Granny Grabbers was having a little rest and recharge in the utility room. She had been working non-stop all day and night ever since everyone had set off for the competition.

She had used every curtain, sheet and duvet in the house. She had dismantled the garden shed, the fridge, the freezer and the cooker. She had obtained navigation and radar equipment on the internet. She had dragged all the exercise bikes and motor-driven walking machines out of the Smarts' private gym and taken them to pieces.

Now she was just finishing knitting an insulated jacket. It was the third she had made.

She heard a very loud noise, looked out of the kitchen window and saw a helicopter landing in the garden in the dark. Hercules zoomed across the grass and over the wall. She had never seen him move so fast.

'Unidentified item in the garden area,' said Granny Grabbers to herself, trundling out to investigate. Her panama hat blew off in a whoosh of air. She caught it neatly in a grabber.

Her child unit came bouncing out of the helicopter, clutching Sir Isaac Newton and followed by another child unit waving his arms.

'I thought your Granny Whatsit was a human being,' Babbatunde was yelling.

'Certainly not,' said Delilah sternly. 'She's much nicer than that.'

Granny Grabbers and Delilah hugged, and Babbatunde watched with his mouth open.

'This is Babbatunde from Amania,' Delilah informed Granny Grabbers. 'We've run away. Babbatunde, this is Granny Grabbers.'

'I am honoured,' began Babbatunde, who knew how to be very polite.

'Good evenings and welcomes,' said Granny Grabbers. 'We've got a real treat in store for you. A once-in-a-bathtime whizz-bang chance to see the world. As long as you like pedalling to add extra power.'

'What on earth?' whispered Babbatunde.

'She talks Grabberspeak,' Delilah hissed back. 'It's all bits of radio and TV and phones and words she sort of makes up. And gets a bit wrong. Have you got a problem with that?'

'No, no . . .' Babbatunde watched as Granny Grabbers set off round the side of the house. They followed her at a distance. 'It's all just, you know, a bit . . .'

Delilah glared at him. So did Sir Isaac.

'Unusual . . .' he added weakly. 'Look, I've got to go. They'll be after me. Police and things. My dad's the—'

He didn't finish the sentence.

They had turned the corner.

Delilah and Babbatunde both stopped and stared.

An aeroplane. A *patchwork* aeroplane was parked by the rosebushes. It was wooden, with bicycle wheels, and covered with a lot of different pieces of material sewn together.

The propeller looked as if it had been made out of soup ladles.

The name *ORVILLE* was painted along the top of the wings in the same red paint the Smarts had recently used to paint their front door. The front door itself, cut neatly in two, was also clearly visible. It was part of the body of the plane, where the pilot and passengers would be sitting, it seemed, on the Smarts' new sofa and easy chairs, chopped about and joined together.

'Of course!' exclaimed Delilah. 'The right brothers, the WRIGHT BROTHERS! The first aeroplane. *They built the first aeroplane.* And one of them was called Orville, wasn't he? She's built an aeroplane called Orville. Brilliant!'

Inside the house the telephone started ringing.

'No time like the peasants!' yelled Granny Grabbers. 'Prepare to pedal! Tickets available for immediate departure!'

She rattled round to the kitchen window, which was open, stuck a grabber through and picked up the telephone.

'Oh no,' said Delilah, in horror. 'Nobody else is supposed to know that she can talk . . .'

She rushed to rescue the phone. But she was not quick enough. Mrs Smart's voice buzzed out, loud enough for them all to hear.

'Delilah? Is that you? We're coming to fetch you. We're on the way to the station now. Your father once got nervous before a competition when he was about your age. His parents had to get him off the church roof with a crane—'

'Thank you for calling the mechanical train information recording,' interrupted Granny Grabbers. 'There are dangerous delays on all lines. Wildy animals. Large weather. Bands of redhot outlaws. Customers are advised to STAY AT HOME.'

She pressed the off button, threw the phone in the sink and shut the window.

Babbatunde's eyes were like saucers.

'She's mad. You're mad. And I'm mad to be getting involved with this, with this . . .' He ran out of words. He stood there, shaking his head in wonderment, his eyes going from Orville to Granny Grabbers, who was now putting on a massive pair of flying goggles.

A few minutes later he had fetched his suitcase from the helicopter and they were all climbing into Orville. Fortunately Granny Grabbers had allowed for the possibility of a passenger, as long as they didn't mind pedalling too. She gave everyone, including Sir Isaac Newton and Dr Doomy, their insulated jackets and goggles.

Dr Doomy was in his cage, which was in a special compartment of just the right size. He held on to the bars, twitching his whiskers. Sir Isaac somehow ended up on Babbatunde's knee. Delilah had the seat directly behind Granny Grabbers. She was bursting with pride and terror. She fastened her seat belt, which seemed to be made out of Mrs Smart's Extra Long Rapunzel Plait.

'Orville will taxi down the road. Take-off will take off at the roundybout. Do not leans out. Little sicky bags for bouncy stomachs.

Sweets to pop your ears,' announced the pilot. She wound up the motor. Then, with charts

and maps flapping in the wind, she steered a course into the starry night.

18

The Secret Island

Early next morning, as the sun rose over the sparkling sea, Orville landed on a little island where nobody lived.

Delilah and Babbatunde climbed stiffly out of their seats. Granny Grabbers lifted three large parcels out of the storage area. These were some of Auntie Tillie's presents, rescued from the garage: a seesaw, a swing and a trampoline.

Granny Grabbers busied herself putting them all up, while Delilah and Babbatunde paddled in the sea. Then, although they were so tired, they played on the presents for a long time.

'So what exactly does whizz bang mean?' asked Babbatunde in an offhand sort of way, because he wasn't used to not knowing things.

'Well,' said Delilah, who'd never had to think about it before. 'Well, it's . . . whizz bang is . . . It's what happens . . . It's how things are when, well, like making Orville, it's—'

'Good afternoons, my name is Grabbers, I will be your waitress for today,' interrupted Granny Grabbers waving two plates of squashed sandwiches and some raisins and seeds and things for Dr Doomy.

'I can't explain it,' admitted Delilah suddenly. 'You just know when things are whizz bang and it's always to do with Granny Grabbers. Like Orville and Grabberspeak and wearing hats and . . . and, oh look, my sandwich has got some gerbil food in it.'

'Better than the new flavour of Brain Food

Biscuits,' said Babbatunde. 'They'll probably call them Camel Sick.'

Everyone laughed, including Granny Grabbers. She sounded like one of those drills they use for digging up roads.

And then something started ringing in Babbatunde's suitcase.

'My mobile,' he groaned. 'It's an Army Intelligence Service phone. It has a very long range.'

Before he could do anything Granny Grabbers had opened the suitcase and grabbed the phone in a grabber.

'Don't answer it!' cried Delilah.

But it was too late.

Granny Grabbers adjusted her enormous sunhat, her massive sunglasses and her fringed floral shawl. She folded two grabbers across her chest and put two more on what might be where her hips were. Her headlamps were bright green.

'No,' said Granny Grabbers very firmly, to whoever it was on the other end. 'Normal services will not be resumed as soon as possible. Healthy experts say children need love, affection, freshy airs and daily relax and tomato time. In future we need more fun and gerbils. Our recipe for today, chocolate cake . . .'

Delilah managed to get the phone.

'My granny says we're not coming back unless we can play every afternoon, eat real food instead of Brain Food Biscuits and go to the park with Auntie Tillie,' she said in a rush.

'And we're not doing any more competitions,' shouted Babbatunde.

'AND,' said Delilah. 'NO WAY is my granny going to be sent to the tip.'

'O is for OK!' yelled Sir Isaac Newton, who was wearing Granny Grabbers' pearl necklace.

'Yes,' said Delilah. 'O is for OK.'

'G is for Geddit!' shouted Sir Isaac.

'Yes,' said Delilah. She didn't realize that

she was speaking to the President of Amania.

Far away, in the Smarts' garden, the President of Amania, who was also Babbatunde's father, took the phone away from his ear and looked sternly at Mr and Mrs Smart.

'Are you going to send Delilah's grandmother to the tip?' he asked, very shocked. 'In my country we do not do this to our grandmothers. It would not be nice.'

'WHAT grandmother?' exclaimed Mrs Smart. *'Granny Grabbers* doesn't count.' And she hissed at Mr Smart, who was standing right next to her in the hole where the shed used to be. 'You see. I was right. Delilah has gone funny in the head. I always said she takes after your side of the family. I should have cloned myself.'

'She does NOT take after my side of the family,' cried Mr Smart. 'There is nothing funny about my head. My hairdresser says it's no laughing matter!'

Babbatunde's father stared at them in amazement. Fortunately for everybody concerned there was someone else there as well.

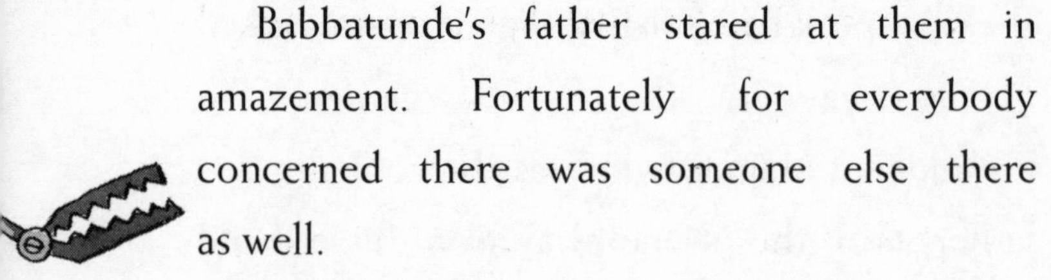

Auntie Tillie took the phone. 'Hello, Delilah,' she said.

'Oh, hello, Auntie Tillie,' said Delilah.

'You sound a long way off,' said Tillie.

'Fairly. Granny Grabbers built an aeroplane.'

'Are you coming home soon?'

'Not if we have to be in competitions and eat those biscuits and—'

'I'll see what I can do,' said Auntie Tillie.

Everyone on the secret island waited. Granny Grabbers passed round more sandwiches, suncream and tomatoes.

Meanwhile Auntie Tillie spoke very seriously and for rather a long time to Mr and Mrs Smart and Babbatunde's father and all Babbatunde's tutors and bodyguards, who were standing around in the garden as well.

When she had finished there was a shocked silence.

She picked up the phone again.

'It's all right,' she told Delilah. 'It's safe to come home now.'

The President of Amania shook hands with Auntie Tillie. 'You are a very wise woman,' he said. 'You have helped me understand that my son is a little boy and that he needs all the things that children need.'

'Don't thank me, thank Granny Grabbers,' said Auntie Tillie.

'I look forward to meeting her,' said the President gravely.

'Oh, for goodness' sake,' said Mrs Smart, who didn't like Tillie getting all this attention. 'You realize that this granny Delilah keeps talking about is just a childcare machine, don't you, Mr President?'

The President sighed deeply.

'I have never heard anyone speak of a

grandmother with such disrespect,' he said after a moment. 'It is clear that Granny Grabbers is a very good granny. I ask you, Mrs Smart. Have we been very good parents?'

19

Safe Return

That night Orville landed in the road outside the Smarts' house and tottered wearily back into the garden, mashing up the grass.

The President of Amania had been called away on urgent matters of state but a beautiful black diplomatic car with smoky windows and a little flag on the bonnet was waiting to drive Babbatunde to the airport.

He shook hand-to-grabber with Granny Grabbers.

'You are brilliant,' he said. 'You have saved me from a lifetime of Brain Food. Thanks to you I won't have to be in any more competitions.'

Granny Grabbers, embarrassed, went backwards into the house through where the front door used to be, nodding and waving and muttering, 'This vehicle is reversing.'

'I don't think that my dad will give up trying to get rid of her,' whispered Delilah.

Babbatunde was shocked. 'But I thought he'd sort of promised not to.'

Delilah shrugged her shoulders. 'He'll find a way. He's like that. He's seen a new model on the Happy Home Robotics website. It's coming out at Christmas. It's called The Nanny Deluxe. He says it's much more efficient and it's better-looking.'

Babbatunde whistled through his teeth. 'I bet it couldn't build an aeroplane. And I happen to think that Granny G is one of the most beautiful women in the world.' For a nerve-wracking moment Delilah thought that she might be going to cry.

Then the driver of the diplomatic car gave a very polite toot on the horn. They were late already and he had instructions that Babbatunde was not to miss the flight home.

'Listen,' said Babbatunde quickly. 'We'll be in London just before Christmas. We always come to see my mum's relations. Phone me if anything seems to be happening. Let me know straight away. We always keep a spare helicopter on the embassy roof. I'll get down here as soon as I can.'

He hurried to the waiting car.

Delilah went slowly indoors. She wasn't sure how anyone, even a person with a helicopter, could stop Mr Smart when he was in one of his moods.

Auntie Tillie hadn't gone home. She was sitting in the living room.

Mr and Mrs Smart were there too. They were watching TV and they were both in a Huge Sulk. In fact they looked very much as they had done for their famous performance as the Ugly Sisters. There were no curtains and everyone was sitting on the floor because there were no chairs either. The cosy rug was missing too. (That had also been used in the construction of Orville, as insulation around Granny Grabbers' battery area.)

'I've bought you this as a present and your mum says it's OK,' said Auntie Tillie. She handed Delilah a mobile phone. 'I'm absolutely certain that you and Granny G are going to get into some pretty wild situations from now on.' There was a terrible crash and a shattering of china from the remains of the kitchen, where Granny Grabbers was, presumably, tidying something up. 'Promise me you'll phone and tell me all about it.'

'I promise,' said Delilah.

'Y is for Y not?' said Sir Isaac Newton, very cool in his pearls, flying goggles and stylish insulated jacket.

'That bear seems very good at having the last word,' laughed Auntie Tillie.

'U is for U bet,' said Delilah and Sir Isaac, both at the same time.

Part Two

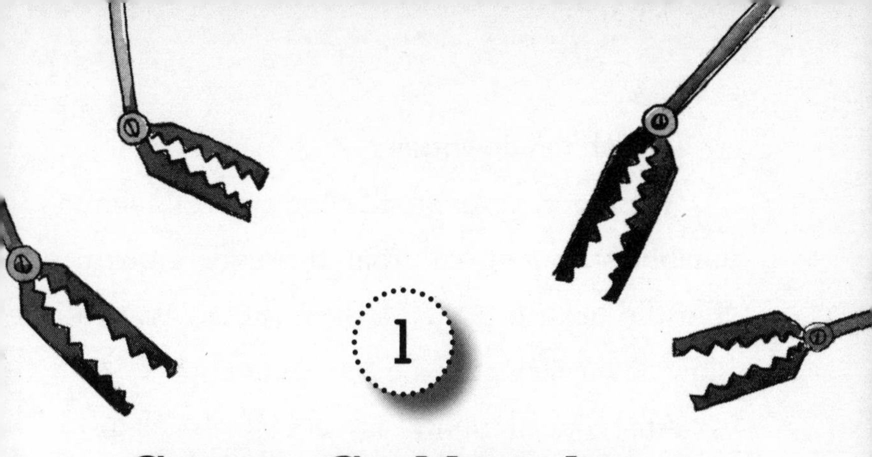

1

Granny Grabbers has a Christmassy Idea

It was two weeks until Christmas. Delilah looked out of her bedroom window. The garden was covered in frost.

Granny Grabbers was skidding about on the icy path. It looked as if she might be trying to reach the washing line. On the other hand . . .

There was a crash and a burst of dreadful language and beeping. Now she was lying on her back in a flowerbed, her little wheels spinning and her six long arms waving. It was difficult for her to get up.

Delilah ran downstairs.

'We report severe road conditions,' Granny Grabbers announced from the undergrowth. 'Hostile ticklish plants. Drivers are advised to slow down, stay at home and eat crumpets.'

'Are you all right?' asked Delilah, almost falling over herself.

Granny Grabbers rolled about and pushed herself upright with her grabbers. She pulled her bobble hat out of a rosebush and jammed it back on her head. The lids on her headlamps rattled. Then she stared very firmly at the roof of the garden shed.

'What are you doing out here?' asked Delilah. It was very early on a Saturday morning. Her parents were probably getting up about now. It would be better if they didn't know that Granny Grabbers was rolling about in the garden.

'Christmassy lights,' said Granny Grabbers in her warm, husky voice. She pointed a grabber at the shed and then at the chimney stack on top of the house. 'Multiple houses in street adorned with Christmassy lights.' Her headlamps flashed red. 'But we will be the most whizz-bang twinkling with the little bulbs, the beardy man with the flying cows and bin bags on the roof and the cheerful white mutants on the grass.'

'Oh,' said Delilah, trying not to panic. Once Granny Grabbers had an idea it was very hard to stop her from carrying it out. 'Er, I think they're reindeer. And a sack. And snowmen.'

'And Santa's Grotty, with little ells,' added Granny Grabbers.

'Grotto,' said Delilah. 'Grotto and elves.'

'DEE-LI-LAAH!' called Mrs Smart from the kitchen window. 'Your father and I are going to the swimming pool now. He needs to do some extra lengths. Then we're going to the Dinky Wrinkles Tanning Studio ready for our skiing holiday. We're leaving in the morning, remember. We need to look our best. And please tell the childcare robot that your father has broken the toaster.'

'I do NOT need to do any extra lengths,' yelled Mr Smart's voice. 'I am absolutely as fit as I can possibly be.'

'Oh, no you're not,' yelled Mrs Smart. 'After you did a hundred and fifty lengths last week you were all out of breath. *I* did a hundred and fifty-two and sang in the shower afterwards.'

'I wondered why everyone came running out of the shower,' retorted Mr Smart. 'And I suggest you eat some of those Brain Food Biscuits you got for Delilah in the summer when she was in the Worldwide Junior Extreme General Knowledge Competition. You still won't be able to sing in *tune* but they might help you to *remember* the *words* . . .

'And I am *improving* the toaster,' he added. 'I am improving it right now, this minute, and—'

His words were lost in a tremendously loud

bang, followed by a fizzing noise.

'Tell the robot that your father has broken the toaster,' repeated Mrs Smart, triumphantly. She slammed the window closed.

'And musical,' said Granny Grabbers, as if nothing had happened. 'Christmassy lights and musical Christmassy songs. From the big loudspeaker boxes.' She pointed at the roof of the house again.

'I really don't know—' began Delilah. But Granny Grabbers was trundling and skidding back up the path, rattling her grabbers with enthusiasm.

They went in through the utility room and Delilah gave Dr Doomy some Brain Food Biscuit. Unlike everyone else, he really liked them. He'd been eating them for weeks.

Granny Grabbers made Delilah breakfast and broke a mug and then Delilah watched while she drew a lot of electrical diagrams showing where the wires would go for the

Christmassy lights. It looked as if there were going to be an awful lot of wires. Now she was drawing what looked like a Christmas tree (grabberdrawing is a bit shaky). Arrows showed which way it was going to bounce up and down and revolve.

'Are we sure this is a good idea?' whispered Delilah.

'Experts report that art and other creative activities are important to a healthy childhood,' said Granny Grabbers. 'Christmassy lights are whizz bang good idea.'

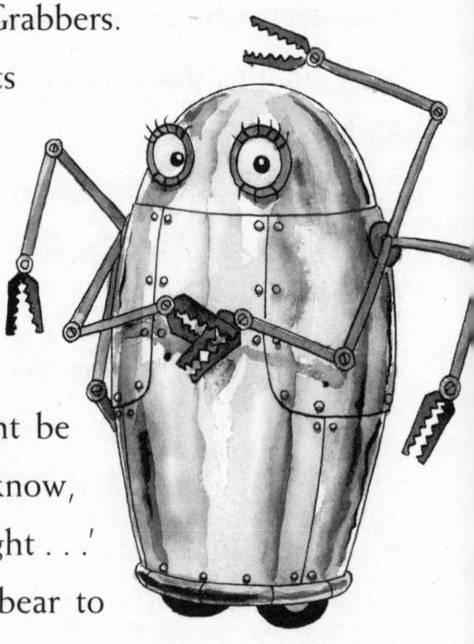

'And what about Mum and Dad?' persisted Delilah. 'Dad might be cross, and, you know, he might, he might . . .' She could hardly bear to say it. 'He might start talking about sending you to the tip again. Or they might phone people from the television and newspapers and things.'

'On holiday falling down mountain with sticks,' said Granny Grabbers. She put her large round head on one side. Her headlamps turned their warmest, most gentle rosy pink. She fluttered her headlamp lids.

'Oh, OK,' said Delilah weakly. 'I suppose not much can go wrong. It's just electricity. And heights. And a very steep sloping roof. And frost and ice.'

2

Dreadful News from Mr Smart

'By the way, Delilah,' said Mr Smart the next morning, just as the taxi was arriving to take them to the airport. 'We're expecting a new robot to be delivered very soon. It's the latest model from Happy Home Robotics. The Nanny Deluxe.'

Delilah stared at him in horror. For a moment she couldn't speak. Then she could.

'NO!' she screamed. 'You promised! You promised you wouldn't send Granny Grabbers to the tip! I won't let you! I'll go to the tip with her!'

'Don't make such a fuss,' snapped Mrs Smart. 'Your father isn't breaking his promise. The old robot will not be going to the tip. It will look after the garden and live in the garage. The Nanny Deluxe will live in the house and look after you. It is a highly sophisticated, *elegant*, state-of-the art robot. We only want the best for you, darling.'

'But Granny Grabbers doesn't want to live in the garden and look after the garage!' exclaimed Delilah, who was terribly upset. 'And she's a stately article too!'

'You're being ridiculous,' said Mrs Smart. 'She, I mean it, doesn't have *feelings*. It won't mind where we keep it.' She smiled at the taxi driver, who was looking a bit shocked at the mention of grannies living in garages and gardens.

'We'd better go now, darling, if we don't want to miss our plane,' said Mr Smart, winding up the window. 'Look out for the parcel, Delilah.'

Then, waving and beaming, they drove away.

Delilah walked back into the house.

Granny Grabbers was standing in the hall. Her headlamps had gone purple with fear. She had heard everything.

Delilah closed the door behind her and they stared at each other.

'Child unit at risk!' cried Granny Grabbers. 'Nanny Ducks will not care for child unit! Will not make healthy eating and shiny teeths! Grabbers all night long in moonless cobbywebs in garage of gloom! Rusty Grabbers! Dampy circuits! Mould will grow on head!'

'No, no, NO!' exclaimed Delilah. 'We'll think of something!'

But at that very moment they heard a van pulling up outside. Granny Grabbers rolled into the living room and lifted the corner of the net curtain with a shaking grabber.

'Events unfolding at the front door. Breaking

news,' she said. 'We advise think of something immediately now.'

Delilah crept beside her. They watched as a man in a red uniform got out of a van with 'Precision Robotic Technology – Working Together for Happy Home Robotics' written on the side.

The man opened the back of the van and lifted a tall narrow box out on to the drive. He carried it to the front step, put it down and rang the doorbell.

Granny Grabbers and Delilah stayed very still at the window behind the net curtain.

The man rang the doorbell again.

Then there was a scuffling noise and the letterbox rattled.

They heard the van start up and drive away.

He had left the parcel on the step. They crept into the hall. There was a card on the mat. They read it together.

Dear Smart Family,

We have great pleasure in delivering your new Nanny Deluxe Childcare Robot.

The Nanny Deluxe is made of lightweight rust-resistant aluminium alloy. She has a humanoid face and two multi-digit hands.

She provides 24-hour childcare and has excellent housework skills.

We have had some problems with the Mark 1, which had six grabbers. The Mark 1 sometimes started thinking sideways. In fact, it has also been known to think in curves, spirals and loop-the-loops. This could lead to Feelings and Ideas.

As far as we know, there is now only one Mark 1 left, a very small prototype, in our laboratory here at Happy Home Robotics.

At this point Granny Grabbers and Delilah both stopped reading and looked at each other.

Happy Home Robotics were wrong. The Mark 1 robot in the head office was not the only Mark 1 left. Granny Grabbers was a Mark 1 too. They read the rest of the letter.

> We are delighted to announce that the Nanny Deluxe has none of these troublesome problems.
>
> She has no Imagination Circuits and only thinks in straight lines.
>
> Before she leaves us here at Happy Home Robotics we fill each Nanny's memory with thousands of pictures of things she will meet in the course of her work. Each picture is accompanied by information about what the Nanny should do. This is called a database.
>
> Because the Nanny has such a big database nothing can surprise her and she always knows how to behave.

> The Nanny Deluxe must have complete control of all household and childcare tasks and is not programmed to share any tasks with any other childcare robot.
>
> Parents have told us that their children have been upset when their old childcare robot has gone to the tip.
>
> Don't worry, the Nanny Deluxe will handle everything. There will only be a medium-sized explosion, a small amount of smoke and some scorch marks on the carpet. The Nanny Deluxe will melt what is left of the old robot into a neat cube that will fit into your dustbin.
>
> Children are very good at adapting to new situations.
>
> Enjoy.

Granny Grabbers blinked her headlamps. All six of her grabbers were rattling with terror.

'Must have complete controls,' she whispered. 'Removal of the old robot will be very quick . . . neaty cube . . .'

'Let's put the box in the garage with Orville,' said Delilah, quickly stuffing the card in her pocket. 'While we decide what to do.'

She opened the front door and they picked up the box between them and carried it to the garage. Orville was in the dark at the back, covered in a huge blanket that Granny Grabbers had knitted for him for winter storage.

Then they went back indoors.

'Mum and Dad won't be back for nearly two weeks,' said Delilah, trying to sound calm. 'We've got ages; should we do some plans for the Christmassy lights?'

But Granny Grabbers shook her head. 'Be alert,' she said gravely. 'Be a very big lert.'

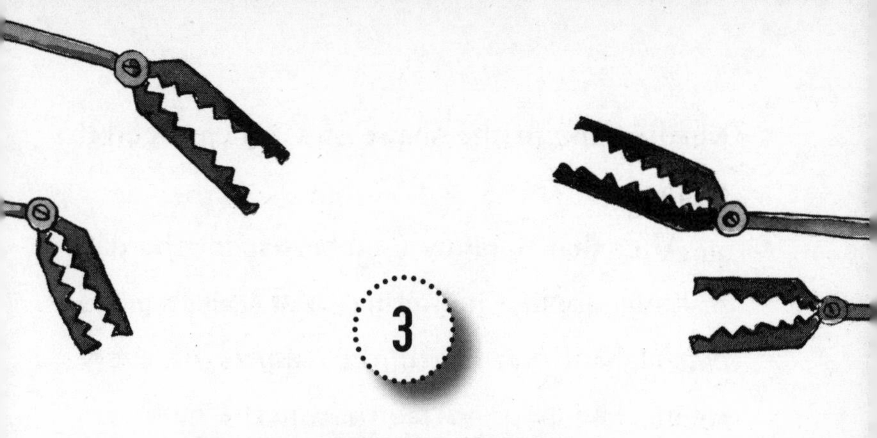

3

Know Your Enemy

The rest of the day passed anxiously. A lot of parcels arrived addressed to Mrs G. Grabbers, Professor Grabbers and, in one case, the Rather Reverend Group Captain Grabbers. These, Delilah presumed, were the bulbs and wires and things for the Christmassy lights.

However, Granny Grabbers was too worried to unpack them. She wouldn't go near the garage. Instead she carried the parcels one by one to the garden shed, which she and Delilah had recently rebuilt. It was painted pale blue and yellow, like a beach hut, and had a little weathervane in the shape of a dancing gerbil on the roof.

After that, Granny Grabbers spent the day rushing about, muttering and beeping to herself. She vacuumed the carpets in every room. The poor vacuum cleaner, which was not at all new, was so exhausted by the time it reached the hall that it started spitting the dust out instead of sucking it up.

Mrs Smart phoned just after tea.

'We've arrived safely, darling,' she told Delilah happily. 'Has the Nanny Deluxe arrived yet?'

Delilah pulled a face at Granny Grabbers.

Granny Grabbers shook her head and drew a grabber across where her throat might be if she had a neck.

'It's not here,' said Delilah.

'Speak up!' yelled Mrs Smart. *'Has it arrived?'*

'It's not actually arrived in the house,' muttered Delilah, going all hot in the face.

'If it doesn't come tomorrow you must phone Happy Home Robotics and say—'

But Delilah didn't find out what she was meant to say to Happy Home Robotics because Granny Grabbers made an ear-bustingly loud beeping noise, took the phone and pressed the hang-up button.

She and Delilah looked thoughtfully at each other.

'They're going to keep asking,' said Delilah.

'Our sources suggest that that is the least of our worrisomes,' said Granny Grabbers. 'Phones can be turned off or ignored. Nanny Deluxe is undispluggable.'

Delilah had never seen her so solemn.

'Child unit must go and have early sleep in case combat begins before dawn,' added Granny Grabbers alarmingly. 'Grabbers is engaged in methodical preparation. Great battles are won by the use of the foresights, the planning and the attentions to details. For the a shoe the horse was lost.'

...e horse?' said Delilah, who was now ...g extremely tense. 'We've lost a horse?'

'Poetry for All,' said Granny Grabbers. 'A popular favourite. For the want of a shoe the horse was lost. For the want of a horse the message was lost. For the want of the message the battle was lost. Old poem. Very wise. All about the attentions to the details.'

Delilah stared at her.

'Also, know your enemy,' continued Granny Grabbers. 'Attentions to details and know your enemy. We must fathom her to her bottoms.'

'How many bottoms has she got?' squeaked Delilah.

Granny Grabbers' headlamps flashed green. Clearly this was not a time for humour.

'Attention to details,' she repeated sternly. 'Grabbers going to do some snacking.'

She set off towards her secret room hidden at the back of the cupboard under the stairs.

Delilah followed, most terribly mystified because, of course, robots don't eat.

Dr Doomy was there in his cage. Granny Grabbers had decided that it was the safest place.

'What do you mean, snacking?' asked Delilah.

'Snacking?' Granny Grabbers sounded shocked. She made a buzzing noise. 'Wrong word identified. Snacking . . . stacking . . . sacking . . . yacking . . . cracking . . . Hacking. Correct word is hacking.'

She opened her new laptop computer and began to type rapidly with three grabbers at once.

'Hacking!' exclaimed Delilah. 'What are you . . . you can't do that, you can't! That's illegal! You can't go using our computer to try and spy on someone else's computer system! You'll get arrested!'

Granny Grabbers ignored her. The words

'Happy Home Robotics Robot Plans' appeared briefly on the flickering screen. Then they plunged into a lot of diagrams and rows of numbers. Granny Grabbers was now typing with all six grabbers.

Delilah was wringing her hands.

The screen went completely dark.

'Now look what you've done,' exclaimed Delilah. 'You've broken the computer.'

But Granny Grabbers hadn't broken the computer. She had broken through the security system of the Happy Home Robotics Company. Now she was looking at their records. (Don't try this at home; you will get arrested for sure.)

A small slender figure appeared on the screen, revolving slowly. Underneath it said 'The Nanny Deluxe'.

Granny Grabbers scrolled thoughtfully down the page.

There was the Nanny Deluxe all see-through. There she was in cross-section. She had only two arms. Her hands were like human hands with jointed fingers and thumbs. She had a neck and a human-shaped head with metal hair. Like Granny Grabbers herself, she had no legs. However, Granny Grabbers, of course, resembled a very heavy metal barrel with little wheels almost out of sight underneath. The Nanny Deluxe was neither heavy nor barrel-shaped. She could bend in the middle, and below her waist she was a straight shiny cylinder all the way down to the floor. Dainty metal bolts twinkled down her front and on her shoulders.

Many, many more diagrams followed.

Granny Grabbers examined them all.

The Nanny Deluxe had no headlamp lids. Although she could speak she did not have a mouth. Just a small speaker in her chest.

She stared out of the computer screen: gleaming, cold and determined.

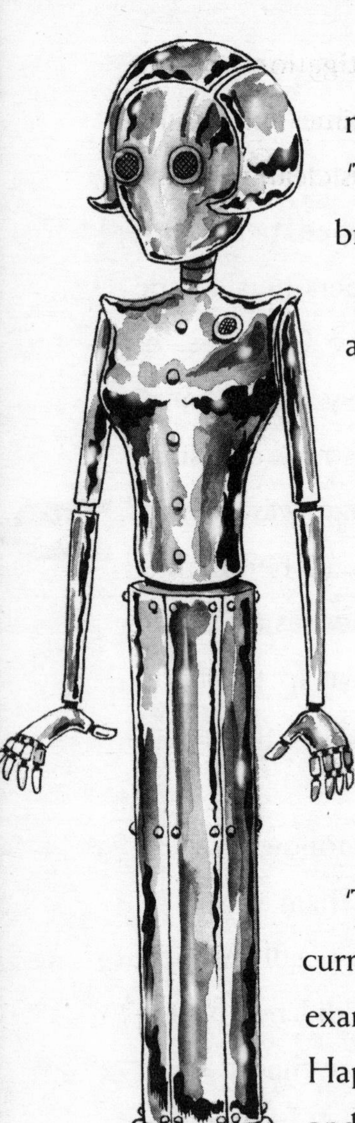

'Happy Home Rubbish . . .' muttered Granny Grabbers. 'Twinky, twinky giant toilet brush . . .'

'What are we going to do?' asked Delilah anxiously.

'He who laughs last laughs biggest,' said Granny Grabbers. 'We are looking for the weak spotty. The clink in the armour.'

'It's *chink*, not *clink*,' exclaimed Delilah. 'Has she got a weak spotty? I mean spot?'

'That information is not currently available. We are examining the secrets of the Happy Home Robotics for clues and will report back in due corsets,' said Granny Grabbers. 'Sherlock

Grabbers will continue investigations during the hours of darkness. Is bedtime. Child unit must rest snuggy buggy. Always clean teeths.'

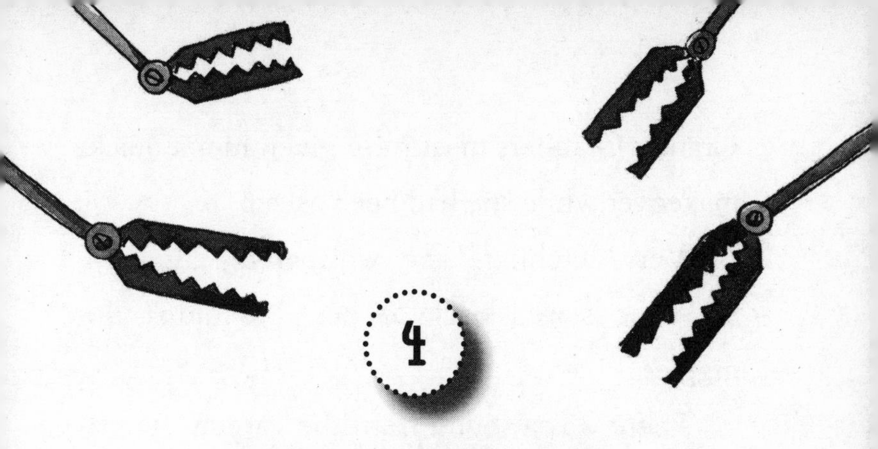

4

B is for B Afraid

So Delilah went to bed, feeling terrible. And Sir Isaac Newton sat on her pillow and stared moodily into the dark.

She woke up in the middle of the night after a lot of worried dreams.

Sir Isaac wasn't on the pillow any more. He was sitting on the windowsill, and he was wearing a straw hat with a flat crown and a very smart black velvet ribbon and an equally smart black bow tie.

He looked like a song and dance sort of a bear. Most unlike him. Delilah realized that

Granny Grabbers must have given him a quick makeover while she had been asleep.

'Very fetching,' she whispered, giggling. Sir Isaac stared back at her. He didn't do giggles.

There was a sound from the garden. A sort of crackling, sparking sound. Delilah crept across the room to the window.

The moon was full.

She could see the side of the garage with its dusty, cobwebby window. Suddenly the window lit up, as if the whole garage had filled with bright-orange light. More light seeped out from around the ill-fitting wooden doors.

And now, unmistakably, there was a sawing noise.

She stared at the garage.

Surely not.

Surely yes.

The doors swung open. Something had sawn around the lock.

A tall, slim, silvery figure glided out into the moonlight. It stopped. It turned its head from side to side.

Delilah saw the icy beams of two small, piercing blue eyes.

She clutched Sir Isaac.

'B is for B afraid,' he growled.

The Nanny Deluxe had got out of its box. And out of the garage.

'Cannot be disunplugged,' whispered Delilah.

She pulled on her dressing gown, picked up Sir Isaac and rushed downstairs. She met Granny Grabbers coming out of her cupboard.

'We saw a light in the garage,' gasped Delilah. 'Then the Nanny thing cut a hole in the door.'

'We must expect attack,' said Granny Grabbers.

'Attack?'

'We must have our wits about,' said Granny

Grabbers, whose headlamps now seemed permanently purple.

'Have you locked all the windows and doors?' gabbled Delilah. She could remember every word of the horrible letter from Happy Home Robotics. Especially the bits about the medium-sized explosion, the scorch marks and the old robot being melted into a neat cube and put in the dustbin.

Granny Grabbers whirred with frustration. 'Locking will not be enough,' she said fervently.

'Can't we just phone the police?' squeaked Delilah.

'No crime,' said Granny Grabbers. 'Just robot.'

'Well, did you find the weak chink?' demanded Delilah. Perhaps the Nanny Deluxe needed huge amounts of electricity when she recharged her batteries, far more than the Smarts could afford.

'Negative,' said Granny Grabbers. 'Still

many pages to go. Our intelligence sources suggest that the invader cannot be stopped from gaining entry.

'Child unit to act normal, be polite and await instructions. Agent Grabbers will lurk and operate under the cover from now on.'

'No!' cried Delilah. 'Let's get Dr Doomy and run away. We can go to Auntie Tillie's house. We can fly there in Orville. Babbatunde will be in London soon; we can phone him, we can go in his helicopter . . .' Her voice shook.

Granny Grabbers' headlamps turned absolutely lime green, their most angry colour. 'Grabbers will not run away,' she said. 'Grabbers will not fly away either.'

Delilah clutched Sir Isaac. She took a deep breath.

'During these difficult times,' continued Granny Grabbers, suddenly sounding very serious, like a royal person at Christmas. 'During these difficult times,' she repeated, 'Grabbers expects all members of the household to do their duty and to keep everyone cheerful and positive.'

She turned her headlamps towards Sir Isaac Newton and stared at him fiercely. Was he supposed to keep them cheerful? How?

Delilah's mouth dropped open.

Then the front doorbell rang.

'We are about to get engaged to the Enemy,' added Granny Grabbers in her lowest voice, a very hoarse whisper. 'Let it in.' She rolled quietly back to the door of the cupboard under the stairs.

Delilah didn't move.

'But I don't want to let it in,' she whispered.

The doorbell rang again.

A very sweet, sugary sort of voice, which sounded almost, but not quite, human, called out, 'Hello? Is anybody home? May Nanny come in, please?'

The voice was so very polite. It sounded

like a bedtime story CD. Delilah began to feel a little bit calmer. They would ask the Nanny Deluxe to go away. They would reason with her.

Or maybe not.

'Nanny was told before leaving Happy Home Robotics that the adult members of the Smart household are on holiday. Nanny is programmed to enter the house and start performing her duties at once. Either Delilah Smart or the old childcare robot must open this door in the next thirty seconds,' said the voice in exactly the same gentle tone, 'or Nanny will be forced to break it down.'

'No one is forcing you, you zombie-faced tinkle-mouth,' muttered Granny Grabbers. She waved a grabber at Delilah, opened the door of her cupboard, went inside and closed it behind her.

Delilah stood there for a moment longer. She heard the muffled click as Granny Grabbers

unlocked her secret room at the back of the cupboard and the quiet thud as she closed that door behind her too.

Then she took a deep breath and opened the front door.

5

A Horrible Bang and the Shut-up Song

'Hello,' said the horrible sugary voice. 'Nanny thought someone was home.'

And the Nanny Deluxe skimmed soundlessly inside, a few centimetres in the air. She hovered briefly, closing the door behind her with one of her two very human-looking hands.

She looked nothing like Granny Grabbers at all. She was tall and slender and silver and as shiny as a bath tap. She even had a waist.

'Are you Delilah Smart?' she asked Delilah.

Delilah nodded.

'Nanny thought so. And the Smart adults are in Switzerland?'

Delilah nodded. She felt very weird.

'And where is the old childcare robot, the one Nanny is replacing?'

Delilah swallowed. She just managed to stop herself glancing towards the cupboard under the stairs.

'Don't you want to tell Nanny?' asked the Nanny Deluxe, putting her head on one side. Unlike Granny Grabbers, of course, she had a neck.

'Let's not worry about it now,' she continued. 'We'll have a nice little chat about everything in the morning when you've had a nice little sleep. Nanny is sure we're going to be very special friends.'

She stared sweetly at Delilah, and Delilah felt a bit like a rabbit being stared at sweetly by a stoat.

'And what is this object?' asked the Nanny,

now looking past Delilah into the hall.

Delilah looked round. The object was the old and loyal vacuum cleaner. It was where Granny Grabbers had left it, by the hall table, and the pile of dust that it had accidentally spat out was still on the carpet beside it.

The Nanny Deluxe advanced. She had put her head on one side and was making a tiny ticking noise. 'Hat stand,' she said. 'No hooks. Wheels. Cloth bag, electric cable. Cleaning machine. Antique cleaning machine . . . Why is there a mess on the floor?' she asked. 'Is this machine malfunctioning?'

Delilah took a deep breath.

'It's just the vacuum cleaner, I'll put it away,' she said. 'It's gone a bit wrong. It just needs fixing.' (Granny Grabbers could fix anything and had once mended a lawnmower using pieces of a microwave oven – although the lawn had tended to look a bit brown after that.)

'Keep back,' commanded the Nanny.

'Malfunctioning electrical appliances can be dangerous.'

She switched the vacuum cleaner on. It made a choking noise and spat out more dust. A small blue spark crackled inside it and it stopped working completely.

'I'm sure we can fix it,' cried Delilah.

'Nanny Deluxe doesn't fix things. Nanny throws them away. That is the modern style,' intoned the Nanny.

She pointed at the vacuum cleaner; there was a blinding flash, like lightning.

Then there was a horrible bang.

The hall was full of smoke.

Delilah crept forward. Sir Isaac Newton, who was crushed in her arms, made a small coughing sound.

The vacuum cleaner was much, much smaller. It was melted and blackened and smouldering. The carpet was scorched.

'What have you done?' screamed Delilah,

although it was horribly obvious.

The Nanny Deluxe picked up what was left of the vacuum cleaner and crushed it into a cube between her two silvery hands.

At that moment there was an explosion of enraged beeping and buzzing from inside the cupboard under the stairs. (Granny Grabbers had always been very fond of the vacuum cleaner; they were about the same age.)

Delilah started coughing energetically to try and cover it up.

'And what is that you are holding, Delilah?' asked the Nanny.

'It's just a bear,' coughed Delilah. 'It's fine, honestly, it's not malfunctioning at all.' She squeezed Sir Isaac more tightly than ever.

The Nanny stared at Sir Isaac Newton. 'Bear,' she repeated. 'Large mammal . . . for example, North American black and brown bears. Can stand two metres tall on hind legs. Do not approach . . . Glasses, to aid reading or long-distance vision. Dangerous mammal wearing glasses.'

'He's a teddy bear,' squeaked Delilah. 'A type of soft toy named after the American President Theodore Roosevelt, born in 1858.' (Something she'd learnt for the Worldwide Junior Extreme General Knowledge Competition was useful at last.) 'They're *pretend* glasses.'

And then something very unexpected happened.

'The sun has got his hat on,' sang a muffled and croaky voice somewhere. 'Hip, hip, hip hooray. The sun has got his hat on and . . .' There was a tremendous wheezing noise. '. . . and he's coming . . .'

Delilah looked around wildly. Then she realized that it was Sir Isaac Newton. He was singing. She was so amazed that she nearly dropped him.

'. . . out today,' concluded Sir Isaac faintly.

The Nanny Deluxe didn't move. She seemed to be pondering some new and puzzling information.

There was a pause.

And a tiny ticking noise.

'Your voice is unusual for a child of your age, Delilah. Nanny thinks perhaps it is a little low in pitch,' she said slowly. 'However, Nanny always encourages children in musical activities. In future we shall practise singing together. It will help the bonding process.'

Delilah and Sir Isaac Newton both remained silent, which was unfortunate because at that moment another voice shouted from somewhere, 'Get back to the boily pits of hell, you sicky smile home-wrecker! Child unit is bee of my bosom! Bondy with her and you die!'

'The sun has got his hat on!' yelled Delilah frantically at the top of her voice. 'Hip, hip, hip hooray!' she started twirling around, holding Sir Isaac like a dancing partner in one of those ballroom-type competitions. 'The sun has got his hat on and he's coming out to-ooo-day!'

Meanwhile the ferocious voice from under the stairs seemed unable to restrain itself. 'And may your circuit boards melt like butter in the big hotty fry pan of vengeance!' it added. 'May your diodes decompose!'

'I love singing,' gasped Delilah. 'Don't you, Nanny Deluxe? I love that song, how does it go?' She had no idea how any song went; her mind had gone blank with panic. 'Oh, you know, Nanny, the SHUT UP song. It goes SHUT UP! SHUT UP! SHUT UP! YOU'RE REALLY LOUD AND CLE-AR! YOU SOUND SO VERY NE-AR!'

Silence from the cupboard under the stairs.

'Thank you for singing to me, Delilah,' said the Nanny slowly. 'Perhaps you could have some singing lessons. I think that would be logical. And now you must go to bed. Nanny will start cleaning and tidying the house and continue overnight. Nanny will call you Deedeekins from now on. A pet name will also help the bonding process.'

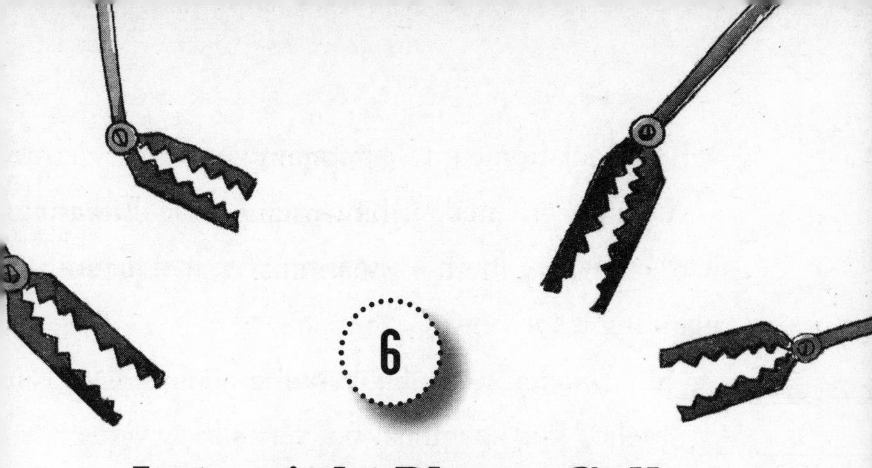

6

Late-night Phone Call Disaster

Delilah closed the bedroom door behind her. Alone at last.

It was the middle of the night now, but she was too desperate to care. She called Auntie Tillie on her mobile.

'Hi, it's Tillie Smart here,' said Auntie Tillie's lovely, kind voice.

'Auntie Tillie, it's me—' began Delilah in a rush.

'I'm sorry I can't get to the phone right now . . . I am walking in the Australian bush. I will be back home on Christmas Eve.'

Delilah groaned. Of course, Auntie Tillie had told her about this trip. She had been planning it for years.

She decided to try Babbatunde's number.

'Hello?' said a familiar, but very sleepy voice.

'Babbatunde!' began Delilah. 'Babbatunde, it's me.' She started whispering very fast. 'Listen. Major crisis. Very bad. Mum and Dad have got this horrible new robot. It's called a Nanny Deluxe. It's armed. It's going to vaporize Granny G. It's got this laser gun thing in its finger. Granny G is in hiding under cover—'

'Hello?' said Babbatunde again. 'Hello?'

'Babbatunde!'

'Hello?'

'Can't you hear me?' hissed Delilah, who felt as if she might go mad. 'Where are you? Are you in London yet?'

The bedroom door opened, the light came on.

'Give me that mobile telephone, please, Deedeekins,' said the Nanny Deluxe. 'Nanny does not allow telephone calls after bedtime.'

'Hello? Is that you, Delilah? I can't hear you properly,' said Babbatunde. 'Your voice keeps breaking up.'

The Nanny Deluxe snatched the mobile from Delilah with her powerful metal fingers. She opened the back and took the battery out.

'You can't do that!' exclaimed Delilah.

'We will discuss this in the morning, Deedeekins,' said the Nanny. 'Goodnight.'

And she went, taking the phone, and the battery, with her.

Delilah jumped off the bed. She jammed Sir Isaac upside down under her arm and ran to the door.

'I'm a little teapot,' groaned Sir Isaac, 'short and stout . . . here's my handle . . .' He yawned. 'Tip me up . . . and pour me out . . .' he added vaguely.

'For goodness' sake, shut up!' she hissed. She nearly dropped him. His hat fell off and then his glasses.

Delilah stopped. Granny Grabbers had said to be polite, act normal and await instructions. It would probably be better not to argue with the Nanny. Also, the Nanny would definitely win.

She picked up Sir Isaac's hat and glasses and sat back on the bed.

'I'm sorry,' she whispered. 'I know Granny G must have programmed you – I mean asked you . . . She must have asked you to be really cheerful. I know you're, you know, trying to help.'

When she woke up again he was lying on his back beside her. She pressed his tummy gently.

He made no reply. Not even an alphabetical one. However, he did make a noise that sounded like a very small snore . . .

7

Top Secret

Downstairs, under the stairs, Granny Grabbers offered Dr Doomy a little piece of Brain Food. Dr Doomy took it in his two dainty paws.

Then Granny Grabbers went back to glaring at her computer screen.

There were pages and pages of secret information about the Enemy, all of it very worrying. So far there was no hint about a weak spot.

It had a laser for disposing of unwanted equipment.

It had super-sensitive hearing and could

travel at thirty miles an hour.

It could see in the dark.

Its memory was so packed with information that it was never puzzled or surprised.

'Thirty miles an hour, indeeds,' muttered Granny Grabbers scornfully. 'How fast do you need to go roundy roundy the house, tinsel-head?'

There was a rustling beside her. Dr Doom had come to the front of his cage again. Granny Grabbers gave him another piece of Brain Food Biscuit.

While dreadful noises of violent all-night cleaning reverberated throughout the house around her, Granny Grabbers scrolled on and muttered.

Then, at last, she gave a beep. Her headlamps flashed red with triumph as she read the screen:

High Security Code 1
Top secret

Granny Grabbers did a bit more grabbertyping.

Serious Problems with the Nanny Deluxe.

Urgent Secret Warning to Happy Home Robotics Offices in Tokyo, Japan.

And then, horrors, horrors, horrors . . . everything underneath was written in rows of little shapes.

Granny Grabbers smacked herself on the forehead in frustration, causing her headlamp lids to clatter down and up again.

She guessed that this was Japanese, and she couldn't read a word of it. She gave Dr Doomy some more biscuit, clamped her headphones over her auditory detectors and turned The Dentists of Doom on at high volume. They were singing their recent hit, 'Spider in your Mind'.

He's a monster, monster spider spinning dreadful dire disaster, making webs of evil, terrible design . . . He's on your house!
He's on your roof!
He's the terrifying truth!
He's the crawling monster spider in your MIND!

. . . screamed the Dentists, accompanied by their trademark drilling noises.

'Any numbness should wear off in a few hours!' yelled the lead singer. *'Don't forget to floss! Thank you and goodnight!'*

(It was a live recording.)

All this normally relaxed Granny Grabbers like a lullaby. However, tonight was different. Tonight she was trapped under the stairs and an Enemy had taken over the house.

An Enemy who was programmed to find

and destroy Granny Grabbers and to steal the precious child unit.

Now she plugged herself into the mains to make sure that her batteries were as charged as they could possibly be, ready for the morning.

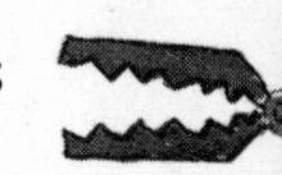

She oiled the joints on her grabbers.

She polished her headlamps.

She had no murderous laser. She had no weapons of any kind.

She was armed only with her mighty love for Delilah.

And she was ready to fight to the death.

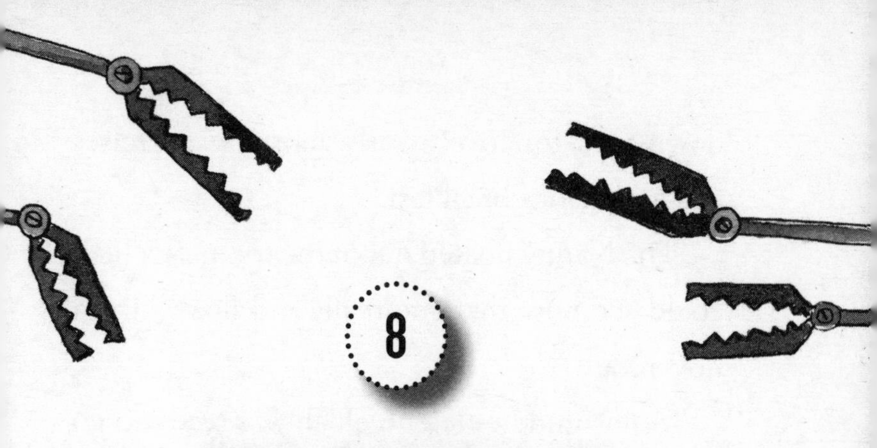

8

Pink Clouds and Smarts on the Phone

There was the click of a light switch.

'Good morning, Deedeekins. Nanny hopes you slept well,' said a gentle, honeyed voice.

Delilah had a feeling that something was terribly wrong. Then she remembered what it was. She opened her eyes.

'Good morning, Deedeekins,' repeated Nanny Deluxe.

'Good morning, Nanny,' groaned Delilah.

'Nanny hopes you had a nice sleep. Please have a wash and get dressed and come downstairs for lovely early morning exercises and a delicious breakfast.'

The Nanny floated out of the room. (Delilah could see now that she really did float. Like a hovercraft.)

A few minutes later Delilah was ready to go down herself. Everything was clearly going to be really awful.

She picked up Sir Isaac.

'If you're happy and you know it clap your hands,' he growled softly.

'Tell me about it,' whispered Delilah.

No time to knock quietly on the door of the cupboard. The Nanny Deluxe was waiting for her in the hall.

The remains of the murdered vacuum cleaner had gone.

The hall table had gone too.

But that was nothing.

So had the carpet.

The floorboards were damp and spotless,

having presumably been recently scrubbed. Several of the stairs, which had been damaged by Granny Grabbers' springs, were neatly repaired with shiny nails.

There was the most terrible, terrible smell of air freshener and the air seemed to be pink.

Delilah sneezed.

'I hope you will enjoy the lovely disinfecting air freshener,' said the Nanny. 'We have Extra Sweet Marshmallow Pink Peach Delight here in the hall, Lemon and Lime Blast It in the kitchen and Moody Mango by Moonlight in the living room for a relaxing atmosphere. They are all triple strength.'

Delilah sneezed again. She had just noticed a number of small cubes of melted, crushed metal near the kitchen door. She recognized what was left of the blender, the toaster and the coffee machine.

The Nanny floated over to the door of the cupboard under the stairs, opened it, raised her hand and pointed a long finger into the gloom.

'Stop!' screamed Delilah.

But it wasn't the dreadful laser beam that shot out of the Nanny's finger. It must have been a different finger. It was only a suffocating jet of Extra Sweet Marshmallow Pink Peach Delight air freshener.

Everything in the cupboard disappeared in a dense pink cloud.

The Nanny closed the door again.

Nothing happened for about five seconds.

Then there was a tremendous burst of beeping.

'You have a very sensitive smoke alarm,' said the Nanny. 'It went off frequently during the night just because I was hammering loose floorboards on the stairs.'

Brrrring, brring . . .

That was the phone in the living room.

Delilah just managed to get there first.

It was Mrs Smart, with a lot of noise

in the background.

'Mum! Can you hear me?' Delilah pressed the phone to her ear. She couldn't remember ever being so pleased to hear her mother's voice.

'Nanny will go and disinfect the kitchen ceiling, Deedeekins,' said the Nanny. 'Bacteria are not afraid of heights.'

'We're here, darling,' trilled Mrs Smart. 'You'll never guess what happened last night! Your father and I entered a general knowledge quiz at the hotel and we won first prize! Aren't you proud of us?'

'Yes, Mum, of course,' said Delilah. 'But—'

'Oh, it was so wonderful to be in a competition again!' cried Mrs Smart. 'You know how we love them! And today we're having a super time. Your father went head first into a snowdrift. We had to pull him out by his ankles.'

'I wasn't stuck,' shouted Mr Smart in the background. 'I was just thinking for a moment.'

'Hans, that's the ski instructor, says I have the most beautiful turn, Delilah,' continued Mrs Smart. 'He tells all the others to get out of the way so he can watch me—'

'He'd get out of the way himself if he wasn't being paid goodness knows what an hour,' yelled Mr Smart. 'You've already nearly poked his eye out with your pole.'

'Mum—' began Delilah.

'Has the new childcare robot arrived?' interrupted Mrs Smart.

'Yes, it's—'

'Oh, lovely! Darling, Delilah says the new childcare robot has arrived already!'

There were some muffled noises and Mr Smart came on the line.

'Have you unpacked it yet?'

'It unpacked itself, Dad,' said Delilah, dropping her voice to a whisper.

'Excellent, excellent.'

'Dad, can you talk to it and tell it that it

mustn't hurt Granny Grabbers. It – it sort of vaporized the vacuum cleaner and—'

'Just put the old one in the garage like I said,' said Mr Smart, starting to sound cross already, despite being on holiday.

'I don't think that would be enough, Dad. It's extreme. It's throwing away all the things you were going to mend like the toaster, and the blender you broke when you tried to blend those golf balls—'

'I was not blending them, Delilah, I was polishing them.'

'I'm really worried, Dad.'

'Let me speak to it,' barked Mr Smart.

Delilah walked down the hall to the kitchen where the Nanny Deluxe was indeed disinfecting the ceiling in a snot-coloured fog of Lemon and Lime Blast It.

'My dad would like to speak to you,' coughed Delilah.

The Nanny Deluxe put the phone to

her auditory detector.

'Good morning, Mr Smart,' she said very sweetly, 'but of course I recognize you. I am *programmed* to recognize you. I am delighted that you wish to speak to me. And, may I add, what a charming home you have and how honoured I am to be a member of your household.'

There was some sort of mumbled reply from the other end of the line. Mr Smart's bad temper had been soothed already. He added something else, but it didn't sound very forceful.

'Unfortunately, Nanny cannot just put old appliances in garages, Mr Smart,' she said. 'Nanny is programmed not to allow rubbish to accumulate; it would not be logical . . . No, the old childcare robot will not be needed to look after the garden. Nanny is programmed to carry out all garden duties to the highest standard . . . There is absolutely no need for any other robot now that Nanny is here. If it is not too forward of Nanny, Nanny would like to humbly suggest that you have a beautiful voice, Mr Smart . . .'

Delilah clenched her fists, gritted her teeth and rolled her eyes. This wasn't going well.

More muffled something from Mr Smart.

'Nanny is not at all surprised that you won a public-speaking competition when you were six and again when you were eleven,' said the Nanny with truly revolting sweetness. 'Nanny doesn't think little Delilah takes after you; she has a very strange singing voice.'

'Please can I speak to him?' squawked Delilah.

'Nanny is so glad that we have sorted everything out, Mr Smart. And Nanny looks forward very much to meeting you in person.' She handed the phone back to Delilah.

'Dad!' exclaimed Delilah. 'Please, please tell her that Granny Grabbers is absolutely not to be *touched*, or, or *anything*, absolutely

NOT *under any circumstances.'*

But something had happened to Mr Smart during his conversation with Nanny Deluxe. He was docile and soppy. It was disgusting.

'What a charming woman,' he said in a faraway voice.

'She's not a woman, Dad,' yelped Delilah.

'I'm really looking forward to meeting her. She seems to know a lot about voice production and elocution.'

'Please TELL her, Dad—' begged Delilah.

Beside her the Nanny Deluxe turned her head with a little clicking sound and fixed her piercing gaze on Delilah's face.

'Well, you know, it all sounds to be rather out of my hands, Delilah,' said Mr Smart dreamily. 'She's in charge while we're away and she certainly sounds as if she knows what she's doing . . .'

'TELL HER, DAD!' screamed Delilah.

'Apparently she's programmed to throw old

appliances away. I mean, we can't really argue with programming, can we, darling?' said Mr Smart. 'I'm just not sure how she's going to fit the old childcare robot in the wheelie bin. Still I suppose she can compress it. And I seem to remember that she's fitted with a laser. It was in the brochure from Happy Home Robotics . . .'

'Can I speak to Mum?' cried Delilah.

'I'm afraid not, darling. She's gone off on the chair lift,' said Mr Smart. 'She needs a lot of practice, you know; she's not nearly as good at skiing as I am.' His voice faded and then came back again. 'I can't chat any more,' he said suddenly and sternly. 'Crossed my legs . . . Got my skis caught in my shoe laces . . .'

There was a yell and a thud. Then the line went dead.

9

The Naughty Lie Detector

Silence.

The Nanny was staring at Delilah.

'I presume from what I have just heard that you gave your old childcare robot a name, Deedeekins. It was called Gabbers. Am I right?'

Delilah stared back at her.

'Oh dear,' muttered Sir Isaac, 'what can the matter be? Oh dear—'

'Don't sing now, Deedeekins, please,' said the Nanny. 'I expect you will invent a lovely little name for me soon. It will help us to bond.'

Delilah said nothing. She could think of

several lovely little names already.

'I am afraid that the Gabbers was very poor at the all-important household tasks,' continued the Nanny. 'Nanny has spent the night starting the cleaning. There were little tyre marks all over the carpets. There was also chipped paint on the skirting boards and door frames where something has repeatedly banged into them. It is a very, very good thing that Nanny is here now to put everything right.' She floated closer to Delilah. 'Now,' she said crisply. 'Tell Nanny where you have put the Gabbers. It is old, it is primitive and crude, and it is no longer needed. Mr Smart is more than happy for Nanny to do whatever Nanny knows is best.'

'I haven't put it anywhere,' said Delilah.

The Nanny put her head on one side for a moment as if she was waiting for something.

'I see,' she said. 'I will ask the question another way because I am sure Deedeekins wants to help Nanny really. Where is the old childcare robot now?'

'I don't know,' said Delilah at once.

There was another nerve-wracking pause. Then a deep, booming, man's voice said, 'That is a naughty lie. That is a naughty lie.'

Delilah jumped. She spun round. She looked back at the Nanny.

The voice was coming from her.

'Deedeekins,' said the Nanny, back to her sugary self again. 'That is the sound of Nanny's lie detector. That is what happens when someone tells Nanny a naughty lie. So you see, Nanny will always know.'

This seemed to be a bit of an understatement. The whole street would know.

Delilah's heart was thumping. Her mouth felt dry. She took a step backwards. The Nanny came closer, looming and gleaming and cornering her between the kitchen table and the sink.

In desperation Delilah had the idea of jumping into the sink, out of the window and into the garden.

'Nanny is waiting, Deedeekins,' said the Nanny, her eyes fixed on her.

At that moment something reeled and

rocketed past the window. It looked like a very large misshapen ball of all sorts of clothes and saucepans and buckets. It was waving a hat stand in a grabber and the hat stand was weighed down with hats, umbrellas and other things that were hard to recognize. It was dragging a big box behind it.

Gaining speed rapidly, it crashed into the wheelie bin, knocking it over, and then shot round the side of the shed and out of sight.

Delilah only just managed not to smile.

'The last time I saw the old childcare robot, it was leaving the house and it was carrying a lot of luggage,' she said firmly.

The Nanny waited. The lie detector made no comment. Behind her, through the frosty window, Granny Grabbers lurched back into view. She was holding the padlock for the shed door up in the air. Some of the clothes had gone and it was now possible to see that she was wearing a cowboy hat. The long grey beard which Mr Smart had worn for his role of Very Grumpy in *Snow White and the Seven Dwarfs*, had got entangled with her headlamps. She snatched blindly at the wheelie bin and began to drag it into the shed. Mittens, umbrellas and a basket of moustaches and wigs fell off her on to the path.

'There,' said the Nanny. 'Isn't it nice when we speak the truth. It wasn't too difficult, was it, Deedeekins?'

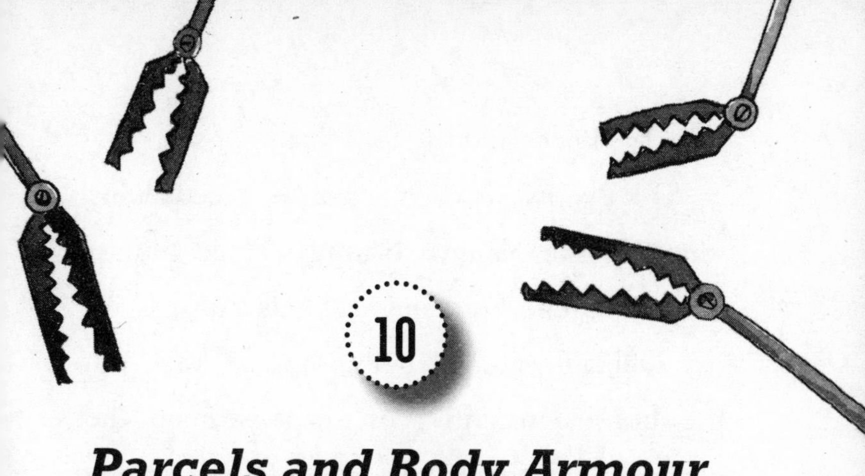

10

Parcels and Body Armour

A few minutes later they were in the garden in the freezing early morning air and Delilah was doing star jumps, running on the spot and arm swings, while the Nanny Deluxe hovered elegantly on the path calling out instructions.

Early morning exercises, she had explained, were part of a healthy daily routine.

'Deep breaths!' she called out. 'Deep breaths! What a beautiful morning! How lucky we are to be out here in the lovely fresh air!'

'Oh yeah, like, heads and shoulders,' growled Sir Isaac from inside Delilah's coat.

'Like the knees and the toes, man . . .'

'Do twenty of each exercise, Deedeekins!' sang out the Nanny. 'Nanny will go indoors now and prepare a delicious breakfast.'

Delilah watched her disappear back into the house. Instantly, or so it seemed, her gleaming head appeared at the kitchen window. It wasn't safe to try and look in the shed just yet.

'Good morning!' shouted someone. 'Parcels for Chief Inspector Grabbers, G. Grabbers Esq., and Madame de Grabbe-Grabbe.'

It was the postman, struggling with several large boxes with pictures of Father Christmas and things on them. Delilah had forgotten all about the Christmassy lights.

'Thank you very much,' she said, as he put them on the path.

Hercules strolled casually out of the shrubbery. He liked parcels.

The Nanny opened the window.

'It's all right,' called out Delilah. 'It's just some things to do with Christmas. I'll put them in the shed.'

'They're all marked fragile,' said the postman. 'Looks like those outdoor decorations. Everyone in the whole road seems to be doing it. They're illuminating their fishpond at number 34. They're going to feed their fish special food to make them glow in the dark, apparently. Should be quite a sight.'

Delilah managed a smile.

Then, as soon as he had closed the gate behind him, she snatched up the nearest parcel and marched to the shed.

Everything was very quiet inside.

She was about to knock on the door, saw the Nanny *still* watching her from the kitchen window and just opened it instead.

Then she stopped in her tracks with her mouth open.

Granny Grabbers was wearing a motorcycle

helmet and her enormous flying goggles. She had a dustbin lid strapped on to her front and another on to her back. Bits of all sorts of other possible outfits were scattered on the floor around her.

'Grabbers has selected suitable clothing,' said Granny Grabbers. 'It is body armour.'

'What are you . . .' began Delilah.

But then she saw something else.

The gerbil cage was open and Dr Doomy was standing on his hind legs on an upturned bucket, juggling three pieces of sweetcorn.

'Did you sleep well?' said Granny Grabbers. 'Have you had healthy breakfast?'

'How on earth . . .' began Delilah. 'I don't believe . . .'

'Our experts here on *Nature with Grabbers* suggest that this gerbil is the only creature in world that can be made more clever by Brain Food,' added Granny Grabbers. 'Dr Doomy is whizz bang with the juggles.'

Delilah came in and shut the door.

'But gerbils can't juggle,' she said. 'They are small, mouse-like desert rodents of the subfamily *Gerbillinae*, which are often kept as pets.'

Dr Doomy dropped one of his pieces of sweetcorn. Granny Grabbers gave it back to him.

'It's not, it's not . . .' began Delilah. 'It's not *normal*,' she said faintly. 'It can't happen. It doesn't make sense . . .'

'Deedeekins! DEE-DEE-KINS!'

'That's her,' said Delilah, still staring at Dr Doomy.

Granny Grabbers clenched all her grabbers into fists.

'I'll have to go,' added Delilah. 'She might come out here looking for me and find you.'

'DEE-DEE-KINS, DARLING! BREAKFAST IS READY!'

'Don't you darling my Deedeekins! Disboard

our vessel, you scurvy crumb!' snarled Granny Grabbers.

Delilah hurried backwards and forwards with the boxes. One had a picture on the side showing Father Christmas with his sleigh and three reindeer, all balanced and smiling, on someone's roof. Another had a label that said 'Extra Large Outdoor Speaker System'. There was a particularly heavy one that said 'Revolving Christmas Tree'.

'Grabbers will be storming the house to engage in one-to-one combat at teatime,' said Granny Grabbers quietly.

'WHAT!' cried Delilah. 'NO! She's got a laser. She's already vaporized the vacuum cleaner, and she's got a lie detector. She asked me where you were.'

'Grabbers will not skulk like scaredy dog,' whispered Granny Grabbers. 'She will not cower in the shed of shame.'

'DEE-DEE-KINS! IS ANYTHING WRONG?'

Delilah opened the door and saw the Nanny hovering on the path holding a plate of something that looked like pancakes.

'I'm coming, Nanny!' she called.

'Honour is at stake,' said Granny Grabbers. 'What use is a Grabbers who does not protect and care for her child unit?'

Delilah clasped her hands in horror.

'PLEASE,' she hissed. 'PLEASE *stay where you are.*'

Granny Grabbers' flying goggles, her motorcycle helmet and her dustbin-lid armour glinted in the dim light of the shed.

'You don't stand a chance!' whispered Delilah. 'Let me do something. I'll phone Happy Home Robotics, I'll say Mum and Dad have changed their minds, I'll pretend there's something wrong with the Nanny, I'll trick her somehow, I'll throw a bucket of water over her, I'll—'

But Granny Grabbers shook her head.

She placed a grabber very gently on Delilah's shoulder.

Her headlamps turned from green to their deepest, most sorrowful blue.

'Grabbers must do what Grabbers must do,' she said quietly. 'Child unit must remember all that Grabbers has taught. She must always eat the green healthy, go to bed early and clean teeths. Regular exercise is promoting the heart.'

Delilah stared at her. Then she kissed her on the side of her motorcycle helmet. Then she went out of the shed, closing it behind her.

She was taking no chances. She very quietly locked Granny Grabbers in the shed with the padlock and put the key in her pocket.

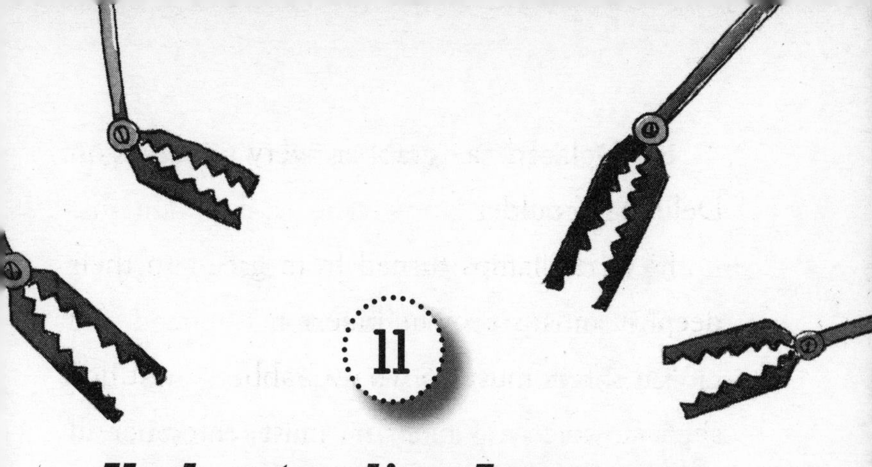

11

Understanding Japanese

Delilah hurried back to the kitchen.

The radio was on and an important person was being interviewed about something important.

'That's a naughty lie,' boomed the Nanny's lie detector almost every time the important person finished a sentence. 'That's a naughty lie . . .

'Eat your pancakes, Deedeekins,' shouted the Nanny, above the noise. 'We have maple syrup, honey or lemon. All my pancakes are made from a French recipe. Nanny has advanced cookery skills.'

But Delilah wasn't interested in pancakes.

'Thank you, Nanny,' she said. 'I am just going to the bathroom.'

She ran up to the bathroom, opened and closed the door as noisily as possible, and then crept down to the cupboard under the stairs.

A moment later she was sitting in front of Granny Grabbers' laptop. Her plan was to email Babbatunde.

The laptop was still on. Granny Grabbers had left in a hurry.

Delilah took Sir Isaac out from inside her coat and sat him on her knee.

'If you're happy and you know it, clap your hands,' he muttered hurriedly. 'If you're happy and you know it, clap your hands . . .'

Delilah gasped in surprise.

The screen was full of Japanese writing. She went to a site that translated from one language to another. Then, with her heart thumping, she read the urgent secret warning from Happy

Home Robotics to their offices in Japan.

URGENT SECRET WARNING FROM HAPPY HOME ROBOTICS HEAD OFFICE TO ALL OUR OFFICES AROUND THE WORLD.

Dear Tokyo Office,

As you know the Nanny Deluxe has no imagination.

She works from a very large database, which contains thousands of pictures of things.

She also contains a lot of information about what the Nanny should do.

We have tried to put everything the Nanny is ever likely to need to know in the database.

HOWEVER, on very rare occasions, we are getting reports of a Nanny coming across new objects that are not in the database.

The Nanny then searches the database for something as close as possible to the new object.

For example.

A Nanny Deluxe took away a lady's lollipop, forced her to accept an apple instead and tried to clean her teeth.

A Nanny Deluxe arrived at a home where there were a number of garden gnomes. The Nanny locked them all in the garage, phoned the police and told them she had captured a gang of dangerous burglars who were armed with fishing rods.

When the policemen arrived she made them sit on something she called 'the naughty step' at the bottom of the stairs because they came into the house with mud on their shoes.

This is a warning to all our offices around the world.

It is only a matter of time before a Nanny sees something that is so strange, unexpected and different that she cannot *find anything at all* in the database that is anything like it. Our experts predict that the Nanny will then become **very confused**. She may run away (possibly for hundreds of miles) or she may self-destruct. Anything could happen.

We are not telling the customers because they might worry. Also they might stop buying our robots.

Good Luck.

Delilah sent an email to Babbatunde saying, 'Crisis. Come at once.'

'DEEDEEKINS!' called the horribly familiar voice. 'BREAKFAST!'

She turned off the computer and sneaked out of the cupboard.

Then, very thoughtfully, she pretended to enjoy breakfast.

12

Carol Singing

'And now we will search the house for insects,' said the Nanny. 'Nanny can spray very powerful Killabug insecticide out of the index finger on her left hand.'

Until it went dark, with a short break for lunch, the Nanny Deluxe and Delilah went round the house moving furniture and looking for moths, butterflies, earwigs, beetles, wasps, bees, flies and spiders, which are not actually insects at all but are members of the Arachnid family.

The Nanny Deluxe was incredibly strong

and determined. She could pick up wardrobes with one hand. She vaporized Mr Smart's most expensive exercise bike because one of the pedals was loose.

Thank goodness Granny Grabbers was safely locked in the garden shed.

They reached Delilah's bedroom at teatime.

Delilah looked out of the window.

The shed had gone.

Without meaning to, Delilah screamed.

'Whatever is the matter, Deedeekins? Have you found a spider?' asked the Nanny.

So far, despite intense effort, they hadn't found anything.

'I'm . . . Where's . . .' gasped Delilah.

'Is it a spider? Tell Nanny at once!'

'Incy wincy spider!' yelled Sir Isaac. 'I'll push you up the spout!'

'Stop that ridiculous singing and tell Nanny why you screamed. Remember that Nanny has her lie detector on at all times.'

The Nanny flung the window open and trained her steely eyes on the dark and frosty flowerbeds.

At that moment a very strange, eerie sound came floating up from the garden.

'We three things,' chanted a hoarse tuneless voice.

There was a pause.

Delilah felt her hair trying to stand on end. She would recognize that voice anywhere.

'Wreck the halls with boils of holly. Fally lally la, la la guitar,' suggested the voice. 'Tis the season to be jolly, fally lally la, la tiddy pom la.'

Another pause.

The Nanny Deluxe had stopped moving.

She made the tiny ticking noise somewhere deep inside her chest. She was, of course, consulting her database.

'Carol singers,' she said suddenly. 'A

charming seasonal custom. We must go downstairs and offer them mince pies and a small financial donation to the charity of their choice.'

'No!' cried Delilah. 'I mean, I'll go. I'd like to go, Nanny. You get the mince pies. Please, Nanny.'

'It is not wise to allow children to answer the door by themselves after dark,' said the Nanny firmly. She sailed down the spotless stairs and Delilah hurried after her.

The Nanny opened the door.

There was Granny Grabbers. She still had the dustbin lids and the goggles and she had added a scarf and six large mittens. She must have made a hole in the roof of the shed and escaped that way; the dancing gerbil weather vane was wedged under the side of the motor cycle helmet.

'Here we come a whatsername,' she said, all

menace behind her goggles. 'Among the leaves so green.'

'Good evening,' said the Nanny.

'Make my day, Nannykins,' growled Granny Grabbers.

'Would you like a mince pie?' asked the Nanny.

'Are you offering?' asked Granny Grabbers. Nastily.

She didn't wait for a reply . . . She raised all her grabbers . . . all six of them . . .

'Six legs! Giant beetle!' cried the Nanny suddenly. 'Insect! Stand back, Deedeekins!'

She pointed at the dustbin lid on Granny Grabbers' chest.

There was a tremendous hissing noise, a huge jet of Killabug shot out of the end of the index finger of her left hand and Granny Grabbers was covered from helmet to wheels in purple slime.

She swayed about, wiping at the front of her goggles with her mittens.

'Quick!' yelled Delilah. 'Get away!'

And still the Nanny blasted Granny Grabbers, the doorstep and part of the hall with the insecticide, which certainly smelt as if

it was meant to kill things.

Granny Grabbers rocked backwards. Delilah slammed the door shut.

The Nanny stopped spraying.

Delilah wiped some Killabug off Sir Isaac Newton's glasses.

'Good,' said the Nanny, all sweetness and calm. 'Nanny knows how to deal with beetles. Now we will have tea.'

She floated off towards the kitchen.

Delilah opened the front door and peered out.

There was a huge puddle of purple slime and some narrow purple tyre tracks leading away across the grass.

But that was all.

'Granny Grabbers,' she hissed into the dark. 'I've got a good idea.'

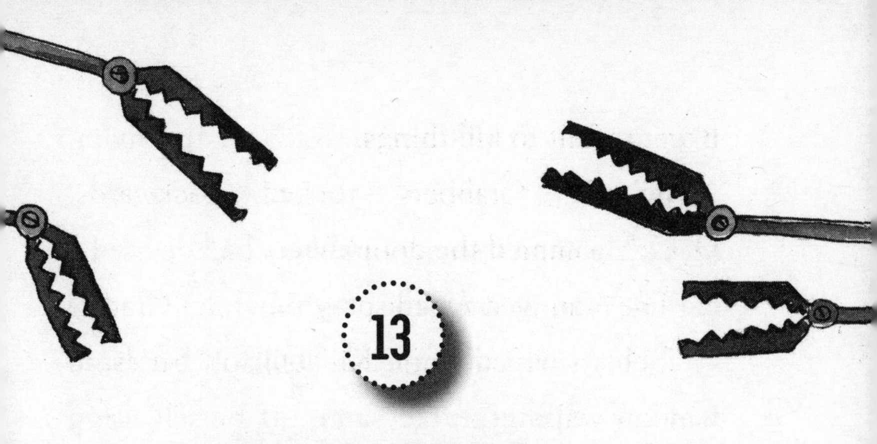

13

The Good Idea (Goes Wrong)

It was eight o'clock the next morning.

Delilah had just finished her exercises. Now she was in the kitchen eating a horrible pancake.

'You know, Deedeekins,' said the Nanny. 'The Gabbers was a very old robot and crude and primitive. It cannot have run away very far. Nanny will search the garden and garage. Nanny is programmed to find the Gabbers and destroy it.'

'Nanny,' said Delilah quickly. 'Would you

like to see my pet gerbil? He's in the living room.'

Delilah and Granny Grabbers had devised a daring plan during the night while Granny Grabbers stood underneath Delilah's bedroom window wiping purple slime off herself using Mr and Mrs Smart's duvet.

It was all to do with the Nanny Deluxe going wrong if she met something that was not on her database. Like a juggling gerbil, for example.

The plan involved Dr Doomy.

The plan immediately started to go wrong.

'You do not have a pet gerbil, Deedeekins,' said the Nanny firmly.

'Yes, I do,' said Delilah.

She had just noticed something outside the kitchen window again. What on earth was it? It looked like a tennis ball attached to the end of a broom handle with sticky tape. The broom handle was wobbling about.

Oh no. It wasn't a tennis ball. It was one of Granny Grabbers' spare optical detectors. She must have wired herself up to it and now she was trying to see into the kitchen through the window.

'No, you do not have a gerbil,' said the Nanny. 'When Mr and Mrs Smart ordered Nanny from Happy Home Robotics they completed a form all about the Smart household. They ticked the box that said "no pets in the house".'

This didn't surprise Delilah. Her parents didn't have much to do with Dr Doomy.

'But I *do*—' she began.

'No, you don't,' said the Nanny. 'Because Nanny is not programmed to know that you do.'

'But I *really do*. My parents just filled in the form wrongly. They must have forgotten about him,' exclaimed Delilah.

'But *Nanny* is not *programmed* to *know* that,'

said the Nanny. 'So it can't be true.'

Outside the window the broom handle swung wildly from side to side. Granny Grabbers was supposed to be hiding patiently in the remains of the shed. (Now relocated, slightly sideways, behind the garage, where it had ended up after she had fought her way out through the roof.)

The broom handle, and the optical detector, suddenly plunged out of sight. Delilah heard a thud and some beeping.

'Nanny is programmed to deal with unauthorized animals in the home in the following manner,' said the Nanny in her most soothing, bedtime-story voice. 'In the case of animals such as elephants, giraffes, lions, tigers, monkeys, snakes and crocodiles . . . Nanny will telephone the zoo.'

Delilah nodded.

'In the case of cows, sheep, pigs and hens . . . Nanny will contact the nearest farm.'

Delilah nodded again.

The optical detector was back. Why oh why couldn't Granny Grabbers just STAY IN THE SHED?

'Cats, dogs, foxes, badgers, squirrels, hedgehogs, rabbits and Shetland ponies . . . Nanny will phone the nearest animal rescue centre,' continued the Nanny smoothly.

'But Dr Doomy is a—' began Delilah.

'*Rodents* carry disease and will be eliminated,' concluded the Nanny. 'Using Nanny's freezer finger. Nanny will demonstrate.' She pointed the middle finger of her left hand at a perfectly innocent tomato on the table. There was a jet of white vapour and the tomato fell over sideways, covered in ice.

'And now Nanny will disinfect the underneath of the cooker,' added the Nanny. And she picked the cooker up with one hand and turned it upside down.

Delilah picked up something too. The

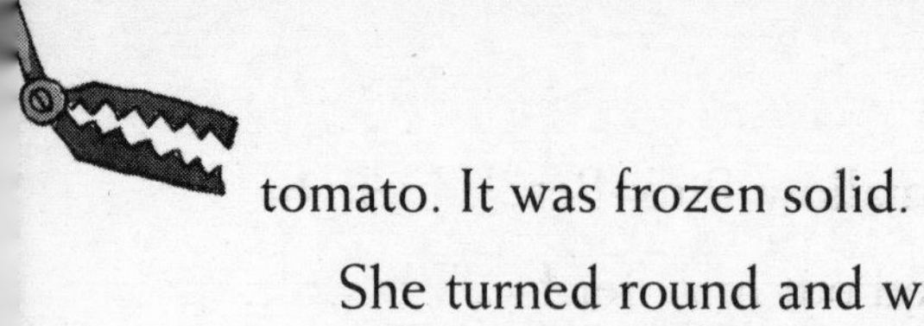

tomato. It was frozen solid.

She turned round and walked as slowly and casually as she could out of the kitchen, down the hall and into the living room.

There was Dr Doomy, in his cage on the coffee table. All ready to show to the Nanny. He was, of course, unaware that he was in terrible danger. He was taking a little break from juggling to clean his long, beautiful whiskers.

'Change of plan,' mumbled Delilah, snatching up the cage. 'I've got to get you out of here.'

She listened.

The Nanny had put the radio on in the kitchen. So far, it seemed, there had been no naughty lies in the *Gardening For All* programme.

Delilah crept into the hall, trying to hold the cage behind her back. As quiet as a mouse carrying a gerbil, she opened the door of the cupboard under the stairs. A dreadful cloud of

Extra Sweet Marshmallow Pink Peach Delight air freshener billowed out into her face.

'What are you carrying, Deedeekins?' asked a voice right behind her.

Delilah turned round. The Nanny Deluxe was not in the kitchen any more.

'What are you carrying?' repeated the Nanny.

'Nothing,' said Delilah promptly.

'That's a naughty lie, that's a naughty lie,' boomed the lie detector.

The Nanny flexed various fingers.

'Show Nanny now, Deedeekins darling. Secrets are very bad for our bonding.'

Delilah shook her head. Her mouth was dry. She could hardly breathe. She thought of Dr Doomy in the cage behind her back. She thought of the tomato, frozen to death in the prime of life.

Suddenly she was lifted clean off her feet by two horrible strong hands. No time to struggle.

The Nanny spun her round in one quick movement, seized the cage and dropped her back on the floor.

'NO!' screamed Delilah.

'Why is Deedeekins hiding this small animal container from Nanny?'

Delilah stared at the cage. The door was open. Dr Doomy was nowhere to be seen. He must have used his new super gerbil intelligence to put his paw through the bars and unlock the bolt himself. He must have jumped down to the floor.

'Well, Deedeekins?'

Delilah took a deep breath.

'If I did have a gerbil,' she said slowly so as not to set off the lie detector again, 'this would be a nice home for it.'

The Nanny's chest clicked.

'Deedeekins has been pretending to have a little pet,' she said suddenly. 'But we must only play with clean, hygienic toys.'

She turned her back, put the cage on the floor and raised her finger. There was a flash and a bang. Then she picked up the tiny lump of twisted metal and crushed it.

At that moment Delilah saw Dr Doomy shoot out from behind the radiator and dash past her into the safety of the cupboard under the stairs.

'And now Nanny will go and check that the old Gabbers is not in the garage or the garden.'

'Oh, *please don't*,' cried Delilah, without any idea of what she was going to say next.

'The bond between Deedeekins and the old robot is very unhealthy,' said the Nanny. 'It must be broken as soon as possible.'

'I-I-I'd really like to make some pancakes,' said Delilah. 'In the kitchen. Pancakes are nice.'

Silence from the lie detector. You can't argue with a pancake.

The Nanny Deluxe stood still. Her cold little eyes had no lids or lashes. They never changed colour. They always stared straight ahead. And now they were staring at Delilah.

Delilah shivered.

'This is a good idea,' said the Nanny suddenly. 'And when it is dark, Nanny will go outside. Nanny will approach the Gabbers silently from behind and destroy it with a single deadly blast. It will not even have time to scream.' And she held up her laser finger. 'Nannykins will enjoy that.'

14

Drama in the Garden

Making the pancakes was terrible.

Delilah felt so worried she thought she might be sick.

Meanwhile, the Nanny kept asking her questions, trying to get information that would help her to hunt down Granny Grabbers.

'Does the Gabbers have good night vision, do you think, Deedeekins darling? How big is it? Is it small enough to hide in the bushes by the gate?'

The lie detector kept going off and the Nanny kept on asking.

And there was another problem too. In the middle of the afternoon, Delilah caught sight of the Gabbers itself, rolling a huge ball of electric cable and light bulbs across the grass, while also carrying a stepladder and two very large loudspeakers. Surely not. Surely she wasn't going ahead with the Christmassy lights *now*.

But soon there could be no doubt. Banging noises started on the roof. With six grabbers and six hammers, a robot can make a lot of noise.

Delilah turned the radio on loud. They had already made lots of pancakes. She asked the Nanny to show her how to make mince pies, and then Christmas cake. Now it was getting dark outside.

Then the lights flickered and went out. The oven switched off. The fridge stopped humming.

'Nanny thinks that there may be a problem

with the electricity,' said the Nanny.

Delilah nodded miserably. She was not surprised. The problem with the electricity was that it had all been redirected to the roof.

Sir Isaac Newton was sitting on the kitchen table, lightly dusted with flour. She picked him up. She would go out there, grab Granny Grabbers and drag her off down the street. It was all she could think of to do. No time to wait for Babbatunde and his helicopter. Not even enough time to get Orville out of the garage. They would just run away. Now.

But the Nanny snatched Sir Isaac out of her hands.

'I is for I don't like you,' he said. Loudly.

'This toy is not educational,' cooed the Nanny. She slammed him down on the table, held up her hand and pointed.

'NO!' screamed Delilah, seizing Sir Isaac back again and clutching him . . .

'No!' cried a small, croaky, beary voice . . .

The nanny blasted the table where Sir Isaac had been. There was a dreadful cloud of smoke. Sir Isaac and Delilah both started coughing.

Delilah backed nearer the door.

The nanny glided towards them. Her headlamps glared through the smoke like evil blue searchlights.

She raised her arm again, she pointed her finger—

Then suddenly something even more important caught the terrible attention of her auditory detectors.

She stopped.

'There is movement in the garden, Deedeekins. Stay here. Nanny will vaporize the bear later.'

In an instant she was at the back door. And Delilah was standing in front of it, still clutching Sir Isaac, blocking her way.

'You will move, please,' said the Nanny. 'Do as you are told. The pathetic Gabbers is out there, interfering with our family life. Nanny will destroy it. She will make it into a little metal cube and we will keep it on the windowsill to remind Deedeekins that Nanny is looking after her now and the Gabbers is never coming back.'

And then there was the most tremendous noise. Right over the house.

The whole garden was lit up in dazzling white.

'Babbatunde!' yelled Delilah.

She opened the door and ran outside and the Nanny came right after her. A helicopter was coming down to land. Everything was blowing about.

'Helicopter!' shouted the Nanny. 'Able to take off vertically! Rotating blades!'

At that moment Hercules bolted out from behind the garage and leapt up on to the wall. Despite everything else that was happening, Delilah stared at him in amazement. He was no longer white. He was bright blue and luminous. He must have eaten some of the glow-in-the-dark fish in the pond at number 34.

'Feline, illuminated,' muttered the Nanny, her chest starting to click. 'Check database. Check database. Illuminated feline.'

The helicopter fell silent and Babbatunde tumbled out. He turned round; his mouth fell open. He pointed at the roof of the house.

Delilah looked up.

So did the Nanny Deluxe.

A giant spider was crouching on the roof. One leg was wound round the chimney stack. Several others were clutching little, squirming elves. The spider had the bearded and beaming face of Father Christmas. There was a Christmas tree on its back, horribly decorated with the dangling heads of snowmen. The back end of a reindeer was sticking out of the chimney.

'Merry Christmas!' thundered the two speakers over the bathroom window. It was

Granny Grabbers' voice, much amplified. 'Merry Christmas, ones and all!'

The Christmas tree began to revolve. The snowmen's heads flashed on and off. The spider/Father Christmas waved an elf in the air. 'Ho and Ho!' he bellowed.

Babbatunde and Delilah grabbed on to each other. The garden was bursting with noise and lights.

Only the Nanny Deluxe stood still, gleaming and silver, her chest clicking louder and louder.

'Father Christmas,' she said. 'Santa Claus, person said to bring children presents on the night before Christmas. Spider, eight-legged arthropod, Santa spider, spider Christmas, eight-legged father . . .' She raised a silver hand, pointing, and Delilah pulled Babbatunde sideways into a flowerbed.

'Kind-hearted giver of presents,' said the Nanny, her voice getting high and shrill. 'Leave mince pie and glass of milk. Do not hang stocking too near the fire. Spider. Spray Killabug. Mince pie. Killabug. Illuminated feline. Glass of Killabug . . .' She lowered her hand. She raised it again. She waved it about . . .

Hundreds of coloured light bulbs were flashing, and Santa Spider's cheery greeting was bouncing off every house in the street.

But the Nanny's voice was louder still.

'Failed database!' she screamed. 'Failed database!'

And she pointed her finger at her own face and blasted herself from top to bottom until she had completely disappeared under a mountain of Killabug slime.

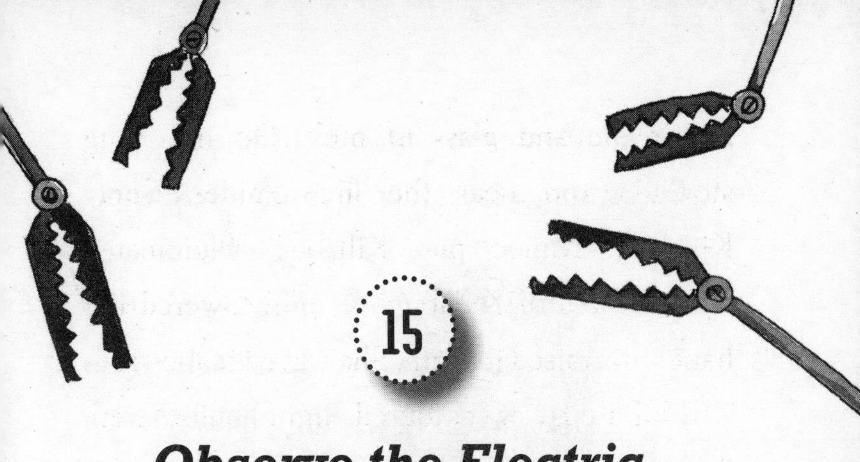

15

Observe the Electric-powered Garden Tool

The Father Christmas spider stopped moving and shouting. All the many, many lights on the roof went out.

Granny Grabbers came rolling across the grass. She had disguised herself with snow (now melting) and pieces of shrubbery. She was carrying four remote-control handsets and a microphone.

She was also carrying Mr Smart's chainsaw.

Babbatunde, Delilah and the luminous Hercules all watched, wide-eyed, as she advanced towards the mound of slime.

Everything was suddenly absolutely silent.

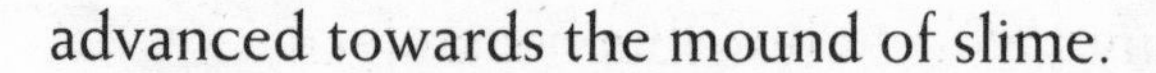

The slime swayed and muttered to itself. It drew itself up and held out a commanding,

dripping arm; it's deadly fingers glinting silver in the gloom.

For a moment Delilah really, really wanted Granny Grabbers to saw the Nanny Deluxe's horrible head clean off.

Granny Grabbers raised the chainsaw . . .

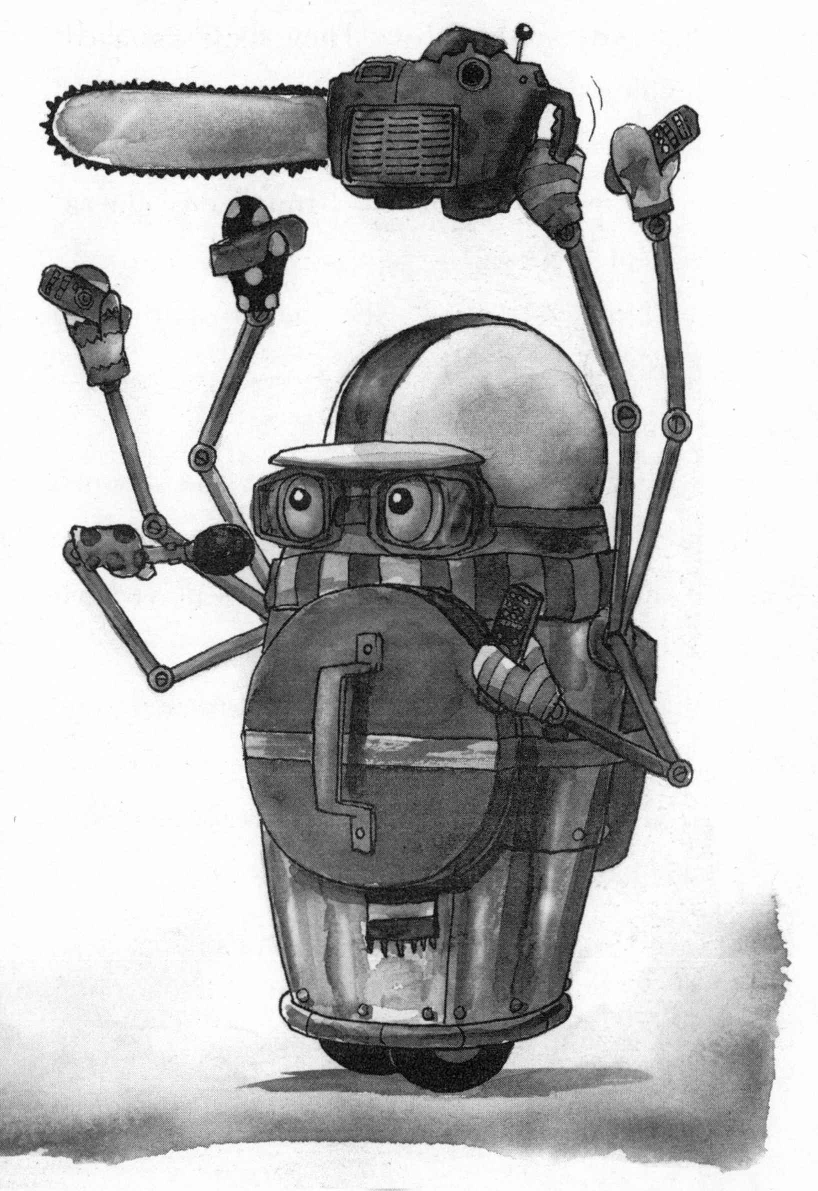

'Granny, don't!' shouted Delilah.

Babbatunde jumped forward and, somewhat rashly, tried to grab the grabber holding the chainsaw. (Never, never try this at home.)

Granny Grabbers' headlamps went extremely green.

'Unhand me, sir,' she said in a low and terrible voice.

Babbatunde unhanded her.

Granny Grabbers reached up and scooped great grabberfuls of slime away from the Nanny's face. Two flickering eyes peered out at her.

'Observe the electric-powered garden tool?' growled Granny Grabbers.

'Displayed in old and primitive second left-side grabber?'

The slime nodded slowly.

'Grabbers could easily extract Nannykins' tinkle-brain circuit boardings and use to decorate Christmas tree. Grabbers would enjoy that. But NO . . .'

Everybody waited while Granny Grabbers removed a twig that had fallen into her headlamp lashes . . .

'Grabbers will not dirty own memory banks with violence. Grabbers follows the Highway Code of Peace. Is whizz bang season of goodwill. Babbatunde and child unit, please fetch the box!'

Babbatunde looked at Delilah.

'In the garage,' she whispered.

They hurried in a straight line over the flowerbeds. It would have been hard to see in the dark but fortunately Hercules came bouncing along beside them and lit the way with blue, bouncing light.

'When Tinkle-Brain gets back to Happy Robot Makers she will be all buttons up and hush-hush about Gabbers,' said Granny Grabbers, still brandishing the chainsaw.

The Nanny Deluxe slowly nodded her slimy head.

'She will speak only of giant beetles and spiders on the roof.'

The Nanny Deluxe nodded again.

'My assistants will now help into packaging. We hope passenger has safe and pleasant journey. Thank you and goodnight.'

Babbatunde and Delilah pushed the Nanny Deluxe carefully into the cardboard box and then Delilah fetched a lot of parcel tape and they sealed it up.

'What on earth are we going to tell Mum and Dad?' whispered Delilah. She was writing the address of Happy Home Robotics on the side of the box in big black letters. Rather reluctantly she added, 'This Way Up – Handle With Care.'

Babbatunde surveyed the dim-lit garden, the pools of Killabug, the extraordinary shapes on the roof and Granny Grabbers' body armour.

'I'll think of something,' he said. 'I like a challenge.'

16

The Lucky Metal Bolt

It was Christmas Eve at the Smarts' house and everyone was gathered in the living room.

Granny Grabbers was rattling quietly about, carrying trays of home-made Christmas pudding and wearing a Father Christmas hat and some holly glued to her chest. Sir Isaac Newton had a robin on his head.

There was a big Christmas tree in the corner decorated with all the normal twinkling things and also some loops of dental floss and individually wrapped cheese triangles. The cheese looked nice but was beginning to smell a bit strange in the heat from the fairy lights.

Auntie Tillie, Babbatunde and his father, the President of Amania, were all guests. (His mother was still busy doing some last-minute shopping.)

Mr and Mrs Smart were there too, of course. They both had something in plaster. Mrs Smart's left arm and Mr Smart's right leg.

They were telling everyone about the skiing holiday.

'Hans, that's the ski instructor, said he'd never seen anything like it,' said Mrs Smart. 'He said he wished he had his camera.'

'Well, I am rather good-looking,' said Mr Smart.

Auntie Tillie grinned at Delilah. Delilah grinned back.

'I was on the chairlift,' continued Mrs Smart. 'I was leaning over to wave to your father, Delilah; he was lying down—'

'I was *not* lying down, I was adjusting my laces—'

'He was lying down *in* the snow, with his legs in the air; he looked *so* funny, people were just *zooming* past him.'

'They were NOT. At least two of them stopped to ask me for advice.'

'Not *advice*, dear. They stopped to ask you if you needed any *help getting up*. You'd been lying there kicking your legs about for half an hour. Anyway, I leant over to wave and the chairlift was very badly designed and my chair started swinging about and then it *tilted*—'

'There was nothing wrong with the design of that chairlift,' snapped Mr Smart. 'You were laughing so much you fell out and landed on top of me.'

Babbatunde, Auntie Tillie and Delilah all burst into fits of spluttering and coughing.

Only the President stayed solemn. He was very good at it.

'My son tells me that he and Delilah had to return the Nanny Deluxe to Happy Home

Robotics,' he said. 'I was delighted to learn that Granny Grabbers will now be with us for many years to come.'

Granny Grabbers lowered her headlamp lids demurely. She and the President had great respect for each other.

'The Nanny Deluxe was really dangerous,' said Babbatunde. 'It destroyed the kitchen table and lots of things in the house, didn't it, Delilah? And you've seen the garden shed. That is the work of a maniac. And the terrible spider-thing it put on the roof! What crazed weirdo would come up with something like that? So different from Granny Grabbers. And then spraying itself with that terrible insecticide. Imagine if it'd done that to Delilah . . . I'm so glad I arrived in time to help get that insane and scary robot back in its box.'

'Well, I'm still going to order a replacement after Christmas,' said Mr Smart. 'The old robot is hopeless. Look at this. I've just found it in my Christmas pudding.'

'In your mouth, dear,' said Mrs Smart. 'You've just taken it out of your mouth. Which is disgusting. I saw you—'

'It's a little charm, isn't it?' said Auntie Tillie quickly. 'A lucky sixpence. People always put them in the Christmas pudding.'

'It is a metal bolt,' said Mr Smart, staring very hard at Granny Grabbers, who was held together with exactly the same sort of bolts at intervals up and down her person. 'And I nearly broke my tooth.'

'It's a *lucky* metal bolt,' said Delilah in rather a small voice.

Babbatunde jumped up and ran out of the room.

There was an awkward silence, during which Mr Smart examined the bolt a bit more and checked all his teeth and then – horrors – Mrs Smart found one in her pudding too. She was just starting to make a terrible fuss when Babbatunde came back, carrying the cage containing Dr Doomy.

'You absolutely mustn't send Granny Grabbers away, Mr Smart,' he said. 'Because she is going to make you famous. She has taught Delilah's pet gerbil to juggle. I am sure that he can be in the *Amazing Book of Records*. Would you like to give us a demonstration, Granny G?'

Beeping softly, Granny Grabbers rolled over to the cage. She hadn't taught Dr Doomy to juggle, of course; it was all to do with the Brain Food. She dithered in front of the cage for a moment. Dr Doomy appeared to have eaten all his juggling corn.

'May I?' asked Babbatunde, picking up the two lucky metal bolts.

He gave then to Granny Grabbers and she gave them to Dr Doomy.

He began to juggle at once. It really was an extraordinary sight.

Mrs Smart clapped her hands. Mr Smart squealed with excitement.

'Granny Grabbers can teach him to do lots of things,' said Delilah. 'If you let her stay.'

But her parents didn't hear her. Mr Smart had gone to find his camera. And Mrs Smart was already phoning the television people.

'My husband and I are very good with animals,' she told them. 'Oh, yes, I'm sure we could teach more gerbils. We could have a gerbil display team.'

She looked over at Granny Grabbers. 'You could train some more, couldn't you?' she hissed. But it was a polite hiss.

Granny Grabbers nodded her head.

'No problem at all,' said Mrs Smart into the phone.

Delilah and Babbatunde both began jumping up and down.

Granny Grabbers reversed into the Christmas tree. The President and Auntie Tillie hugged each other. Granny Grabbers hugged Sir Isaac Newton.

'And a Merry Christmas, One and All,' he said, spitting out bits of holly.

Acknowledgements

Thank you for everyone who has been involved in the preparation of this book.

At AP Watt – Caradoc King, Louise Lamont, Elinor Cooper and Hattie Thorowgood.

At Hodder Children's Books – Beverley Birch, Naomi Pottesman, Chris Fraser and to Hazel Cotton and Sarah Taylor-Fergusson.

To Pete Williamson for his brilliant illustrations.

To J Salieri for editorial comment, early sketches for Granny Grabbers and design ideas.

To Ian Gundy, Rick Adair, Claire Foster and Jules Burt for their advice on signing events.

Many thanks to Alan Darke, recently of Buttle UK, with every good wish to him and his family for a long, busy and happy retirement.

Many thanks also to Joe Turner for his kind generosity and to Rosemary and Trevor Whitbread, patrons of the arts.

And finally, much thanks to the staff at The Ferns. Nil satis nisi optimum.

Coming soon . . .

GRANNY GRABBERS'

Daring Rescue

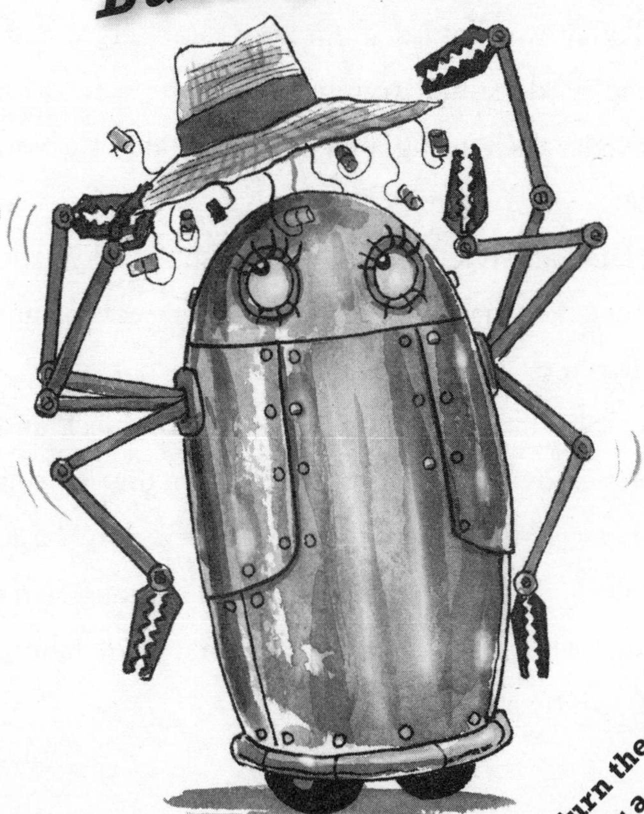

Turn the page for a sneak peek

Today was Saturday. Granny Grabbers was in the garden shed trying to learn how to do a magic trick using playing cards and sleeves. She was wearing a top hat and a special magician-style jacket which she had made herself. It had six sleeves, one for each of her grabbers, and lots of secret pockets.

She had a round head, no visible neck and her body was barrel-shaped, with tiny wheels underneath and she looked like a very large purple ball covered in stars. The magician's coat was much too big. The hat kept falling down over her headlamps.

Now she couldn't remember where she'd hidden the card. It could be in a sleeve. Or perhaps it was in a secret pocket.

Dr Doomy the gerbil watched her politely.

'This your card?' Granny Grabbers asked in her warm voice. She stuck a grabber in a sleeve and produced an egg whisk. This had nothing to do with the magic trick and must have been left over from breakfast.

Dr Doomy put his head on one side. He was a very clever gerbil and he knew the difference between the King of Hearts and a kitchen utensil.

At that moment Delilah opened the door of the shed.

'Child Unit reverse!' commanded Granny Grabbers. 'Private magical practice!'

Delilah reversed.

'Is *this* your card?' Granny Grabbers asked Dr Doomy sternly.

He twitched his whiskers. She had pulled a

squashed looking lettuce from somewhere deep in one of her armpits.

'Can I come in now?' called Delilah.

'More practice to make perfects,' muttered Granny Grabbers, giving Dr Doomy some of the lettuce. She took off the top hat and the King of Hearts fell out on to the floor. Then she started trying to take off the magician's jacket. She didn't usually wear clothes and certainly nothing with sleeves. Hats were ok, and gloves and scarves . . . but this . . .

'Are you OK?' called Delilah anxiously. She could hear a lot of grumbling and beeping. Then scuffling, a crash and much ruder grumbling getting louder and louder. The shed door flew open and Granny Grabbers toppled out all tangled up in sparkly material and with three sleeves accidentally knotted over her head.

'Urgent backup assistance needed,' she announced. She started to roll down the path, beeping and snatching at things with a free grabber. Then she hit a hedge and became stuck there.

Delilah picked up the top hat and ran after her. 'Granny G,' she gasped, 'there's going to be something on TV about some robots from Happy Home Robotics.'

Granny Grabbers stood up carefully. She swivelled her round head from side to side. She saw through her optical detectors, which were in the middle of her two headlamps. They looked like very large eyes. Now she tested her fringed headlamp lids, rattling them up and down. Then she flexed each grabber in turn. Delilah untangled the sleeves of the sparkly coat and gave her back her hat.

'No damage detected,' said Granny Grabbers. 'Normal service is now resumed.'

Mr and Mrs Smart were sitting in the living room watching the television sideways. They were watching it sideways because they were practising their arm wrestling and they were doing that because they were in training for the 'His and Hers Arm-wrestling and Head Standing Competition' which was held every year at the Big Brains Institute where they worked.

'I'm not really trying,' Mr Smart was saying. 'If I tried I'd win straight away. It wouldn't be fair.'

His face was bright red. Sweat was all over it.

'I'm not really trying either,' said Mrs Smart, gritting her teeth and scrunching her eyes.

They were both too busy not trying, to notice Delilah and Granny Grabbers creep and rattle into the room and settle down on and beside the sofa.

'Blingman's Department Store opened six months ago. It's the newest, biggest and most expensive store in the city,' yelled a reporter, who seemed to be standing in a car park somewhere in a strong wind.

'Blingman's have had their fair share of mysterious problems since they opened. Including a haunted lift, would you believe. But it's all good news today. The owner, Buzz Blingman, has allowed us up here on to the roof to see something you *won't* see looking around the store. No, not a beautiful display of jewellery or furnishings, although you'll find all that and more downstairs. No, We're here to see the *cleaners*.'

She was fighting with the wind. Her hair was blowing in all directions. The papers she was holding kept flapping into her face.

'This is the Sort It Squad. The new robotic cleaning personnel made by Happy Home Robotics. They're going to be doing all the cleaning in this massive five-storey building. And believe me, when you've seen them on parade you are going to be very, very impressed.'

Safe in the Smarts' living room Granny Grabbers and Delilah held hand to grabber. Happy Home Robotics had made Granny Grabbers. But that was a long time ago. After that they'd made a lot of other robots, including the terrifying, shiny, two-armed, gliding, talking, laser-fingered Nanny DeLuxe. Mr Smart had tried to replace Granny Grabbers with a Nanny Deluxe. It had been a time of ugliness and pain.

Even now, if Mr and Mrs Smart ever found out that Granny Grabbers had feeling and ideas of her own they would send her back to Happy Home Robotics to be re-programmed. Robots were not supposed to have feelings and ideas. (They also didn't know that she could talk.)

'What you inventing now you monster factory,' whispered Granny Grabbers, staring ferociously at the screen.